WITHDRAWN

**Xavier's Folly
and Other Stories**

Xavier's Folly
and Other Stories

Max Evans

UNIVERSITY OF NEW MEXICO PRESS
Albuquerque

PS
3555
.V23
X3
1984

Library of Congress Cataloging in Publication Data

Evans, Max.
  Xavier's folly, and other stories.

  Contents: Xavier's folly—One-eyed sky—Candles in the bottom of the pool.
  I. Title.
PS3555.V23X3   1984   813'.54   83-25907
ISBN 0-8263-0700-0

© 1962, 1972, 1973 by Max Evans. All rights reserved.

Contents

Xavier's Folly   1

One-Eyed Sky   37

Candles in the Bottom of the Pool   67

Xavier's Folly

1

The creature moved across the hill, struggling through the thick black grass with determination. Xavier Del Campo opened his eyes a little more and watched the bug straining through the jungle of hair on his heavy arm. The sun formed tiny prisms of light here and there. He imagined they were shining on a vast stage and he could see Tamara, the great Russian ballet star, pirouetting under their golden glow. He could hear the music, especially the strings, and then she finished. The applause shook rocks loose in the earth. She was beckoning him to come and share her glory on the stage. Imagine!

Xavier lifted his head from his arms and slowly sat up, rubbing the heavy curled hair on his head. He stared off at the blue hump of the Rocky Mountains rising like prehistoric monsters out of the earth. His eyes looked above them into the sky. He liked to look at a cloudless sky since he discovered that it was full of holes. He was entranced by the firmament. The holes pulsated with greens, pinks and purples. He felt sorry for people who just saw the sky as a blue curtain. They were missing so much. All they had to do was really look. That's all.

His wife was one of those who missed. Shortly after they were married he was pursuing his hobby of 'sky staring' when she stepped out of the house to hang out the wash. She asked, as she walked past him, "An eagle?" When he didn't answer, she asked, "A hawk?"

"Look at the sky," he said, "it's full of pretty holes."

She cast a suspicious eye upon him. Seeing he was serious, she snorted. "It's your brain that's full of holes."

Their relationship had deteriorated after that. His great Mexican eyes dropped back down to the sage-covered foothills of the mountains. He could see their little house and sheds there. Lonely. Aloof. He tried not to think of her but it was no use. Tonight he had to tell her of his great plan. A feeling of dread caressed his short, muscled body. He stood up and looked at the ditch in front of him. Manuel usually dug the ditches while Xavier tended to the fitting of pipes. He didn't mind digging, but it took up valuable time. As a plumber, Xavier was an artist. All metal fit perfectly and was sealed the same. He was immensely proud that his pipes never leaked. Never. Now, however, he must dig. Yesterday he paid Manuel so it was reasonable to figure that today he was drunk. Xavier might have joined him but he had to save money. It would take a lot of cash to fulfill his plan. He already had thirty-seven hundred dollars hidden in a bucket behind the outdoor privy.

He lifted the pick from the loose dirt and stepped into the ditch to dig. The steel point pierced the earth and bit away chunks as he swung up and down in powerful rhythms. The spring air was not hot, but sweat soon darkened the underarms of his shirt. When had he promised his clients to have the plumbing installed? They came every day from town to check on his progress. They were anxious to move into their new adobe. It was expensive living in a hotel, they informed him.

Xavier swung faster and harder at these thoughts. Today, though, they failed to come and he dug straight till dark, almost finishing the ditch. He dug it over three feet deep so the harsh winters could never freeze the pipes. All his customers complained at his seeming slowness, but later they commented on the perfection of his skill and recommended him to others. He was never without work.

When he could no longer see clearly what he was doing he dropped the pick, got in his faded old red truck and headed home. It had to be tonight. Yes, he had to tell her now. He took a short cut around the town of Ragoon, chugging into the foothills towards the light in the window that glowed deceivingly warm. A coyote loped across the winding road in front of him, glancing sideways, and vanished in the sage and darkness.

The two old cur dogs moved off the porch and barked a half-hearted welcome. As he got out of the truck the dogs smelled his legs and waved their tails so slightly it was only a suggestion. He thought that somehow they had adopted a certain attitude of their mistress.

As he opened the door he wondered why he didn't feel that contentment that men were supposed to feel on the return to the hearth. Where was the surging pride in a hard day's work to share with his lady?

XAVIER'S FOLLY

She and her two daughters were just finishing the evening meal. One girl was fourteen, the other sixteen—Suzanne and Suzette. They had the same gray eyes of their mother, watery, dull and somehow appearing a bit out of focus. They moved these orbs slightly upward in greeting. Both had buck teeth and when they smiled their lips pulled back and a wad of flesh wrinkled up over the gums. It had come to Xavier on occasion that their mouths reminded him of a mule's behind when he strained to pull a deep plow through dry earth. He had long been curious as to what their real father looked like. But he would never know for the man had died years before, from the bellyache. Xavier would soon understand more about his demise.

Marion looked up, saying between chews of spaghetti, "You're late. We went ahead and ate."

"Aw, that's all right. I'm not very hungry anyway." He washed his face and hands in a tin pan of cold water and sat down. The girls got up and went to their room. He watched them go, shaking their rounded tails far more than the dogs. He reached for the bowl and took the little bit of spaghetti left. As he buttered a cold biscuit, she poured him a cup of warm black coffee. He ate. She sat.

He knew exactly what she'd say when she did speak.

"When are you gonna finish the Bently job?"

"Next week if Manuel gets over his cold."

"Cold? He's too full of wine to catch anything. You said you'd put in our plumbing when the Bently job is done."

He took a long drink of coffee and tried very hard to see out through the old adobe wall. In fact, he tried to *be* outside. It didn't work.

"You been sayin' you was gonna put in our plumbin' after

every job for a year now. It's gettin' embarrassin' to explain to folks. The girls are ashamed to bring company home. How can they explain to their friends that they have to go outside to the toilet? Some plumber you are."

Xavier never knew why he said it. The statement was against his nature and made his important announcement much more difficult,

"It's cleaner to crap outside."

He knew he'd stepped over the bounds with her. When she was mad she pulled at her stringy, mouse-colored hair and squinted her eyes. She was pulling and squinting right now.

"You tryin' to get funny with me or sumpthin'?"

"Marion, I got something important to tell you."

"You tryin' to get funny, huh?"

"Marion, I . . ."

She got up from the table and started gathering the dirty dishes. She took his coffee before he was half through and made a lot of noises doing all this.

"You smell."

"Smell what?" he asked.

"You. You, that's what. You smell like a boar hog. If you'd put a bath in at least you could take a shower before settin' down at the table with us."

"I'll take a tub bath tonight," he placated, "but first I want to tell . . ."

"Imagine havin' to bathe in that old tin washtub. A plumber's wife. Jist imagine," she said.

"Now, Marion, I promise. I'll even promise on a Bible." He walked over and got the book out of a dresser drawer to show faith. "Now see here, I got my hand on this Bible."

She stopped washing dishes and glared at him. "Well?" she said, waiting, almost believing him now.

"All right now. I promise on the word of the Lord that as soon as I put on my ballet presentation I'll put in the plumbing."

"Your what?" she shrieked.

"The great Tamara. I'm going to bring her to Ragoon. I'm going to present her."

Marion just stood and squinted till he couldn't even see her eyes, only a tiny thin line where they had been. She was almost pulling her stringy mouse-colored hair out by the shallow roots. What poor Xavier didn't know was that Marion had married him to get her plumbing installed. She had always intended to kick him out just as soon as that was accomplished.

Finally she said in a deadly flat tone, "I always knew you was crazy. I knew it from the first time you was tryin' to find holes in the sky. Ballet? Ballet? My God! I ought to have you locked up!"

"But . . . but ballet is beautiful."

"My God! There ain't anybody in Ragoon that even knows how to spell the word. Beautiful my wild ass."

Xavier rubbed at his curly hair and twisted around on his feet still holding the Bible as if God himself might just materialize from the pages and smight him dead. His stomach hurt. How was he going to make her understand?

"Just because folks don't know is no reason that they can't learn to like beautiful things."

She hurled the dish towel across the room and sat down on the battered-up divan. "Beautiful. Beautiful, he says. All I ever want in the world to make it beautiful is a bathroom and now you tell me that I have to wait while you bring a bunch of idiots here to dance around on their toes. I'm tellin' you, you even bring it up and the people of Ragoon'll laugh you plumb into Texas. My God! Toe dancing! People never was meant to dance on their toes. They might as well try swingin' from their tails like monkeys."

She got up and went in to talk to her daughters. He could hear sounds from the room, but he couldn't make out the words. For this he was thankful. He got himself a cup of cold coffee and sat down trying to think.

She came out slamming the door with a victorious air about her sagging breasts. She stopped in the middle of the floor, her feet spread apart like a boxer's, and said, "You know what we're gonna do?"

He looked up at her, knowing that whatever they were going to do would not be to his benefit.

"We're going into town first thing in the mornin' and we're gonna draw ever dime out of the bank." She smiled now like a coyote with a rabbit by the hind-quarters. "And we're gonna hire Ben Gonzales to put in our plumbin'. There won't be no cockeyed ballet, no nothin'." She paused, relishing the sad look on Xavier's face, and then threw the coup de grace at him. "Now won't the folks of Ragoon get one hell of a laugh outa the fact your competitor is puttin' in *our* plumbin'? Huh?"

Things didn't get any better that night. Xavier had his choice of sleeping on the divan, which had springs that punched one's body, or sleeping out back in a shed with the goats. He wrapped up in an old rag rug and said to the goats,

"Don't worry, it's just for tonight."

Marion lay in bed and exulted over her move. Not only would she make a laughing stock out of Xavier but she'd run him off as soon as the plumbing was installed. She had recently learned that the useless looking sagebrush land her first husband had left her could be turned into a housing development. At least that marriage had paid off. The land ran all the way into the timber on the mountains. The realtors told her she would make a fortune, but it would take time. In the meanwhile she'd get her bathroom and then run Xavier off before he could share the benefits from any real estate profits. Marion was a lady who made plans.

Out back with the goats, Xavier thought of himself as a coward. He just couldn't muster up the guts to tell her there was only four dollars and thirteen cents in the bank. But with all his immediate troubles, and the fact he'd been demoted to the animal shelter for the night, he dreamed big dreams.

Xavier's mother and father drowned in a flash flood when he was ten years old. He was sent to live with an uncle and aunt in Los Angeles. His uncle was a plumber and Xavier was apprenticed. He learned how to cut and thread pipe; how to measure and fit; how to melt the lead and permanently seal the joints. He learned fast. The first two years he went to public school, but then he had to quit because he became too valuable to his uncle to be wasted on reading and writing.

They lived upstairs in a very crowded section of old houses. At night, after helping his aunt do the supper dishes, he'd sit out on the walk-up porch, look at the city and conjure up visions of all the things the millions of people were doing at that moment.

Across an alley was an empty-looking old building. One night a light beamed from the big window and there for the first time he saw ballet. A lady had opened a dance academy.

At first, Xavier thought their actions very strange and foolish, but each night he was drawn back to watch. Gradually he began to feel the grace and dignity, and finally he had the courage to slip down to the window for a closer look. He was entranced.

There was one long-haired girl who looked to be of his own blood—Mexican. She seemed to float when she leaped. He kept hoping that she would truly learn to fly with a hawk. Each time she danced, his muscles twitched in his short frame with her and for her. He fell in love with her; he fell in love with the dance. A thirst was upon him. Oh, he didn't deceive himself that *he* would ever dance. Not with his build. He would simply look like a fat rubber ball bouncing about. No, he participated with his soul.

Finally a night came when all the parents arrived to see the results of their money and their children's dedication. Xavier had saved pennies for weeks so he could attend. His uncle laughed but his aunt smiled, somehow knowing.

When the lights came on and the long-haired girl was spotlighted, he thought he'd faint it was so lovely. As she danced in the dark with the light following, it became a glorious, sensuous thing to Xavier. He felt that he himself was the light and that he completely enveloped her while she moved with the grace of a Maltese cat.

He waited outside that night as the people left chattering

with their children and friends. When she came out (he never remembered her name) he touched her on the arm and said,

"You . . . you are beautiful."

She stunned him with a smile that radiated right straight through his heart. Then he ran.

2

Xavier was grown now. He was a master plumber. He had returned to his own beloved Southwest and started a business in Ragoon. Then one day a movie called RED SHOES came to town. It was an old and timeless film. Never, not even in Los Angeles, had he seen anything so hypnotic. The dark, flame-lit red hair of Moira Shearer floated with her like thousands of tiny writhing snakes. Her white face and body were from other planes; they were from heaven. When she had thrown herself from a window in front of the train, he'd died with her! And when the camera had shown the red satin shoes and the pink tights with the blood coming through, he'd died a thousand times more. But even so . . . What a film! What a lady! What a dance! Finally he knew what the word "magic" really meant. It meant ballet.

Later he saw a photographic study of Tamara in a national magazine. He looked at it until the pages were worn and shredded. He knew now what he must do. He knew what he was born for—his whole purpose. He would die to accomplish it. He would bring the great Tamara here to Ragoon and present her. He could see it now: XAVIER PRESENTS.

He had already started saving his money for this dream when he met Marion. She had seemed so sweet when she invited him up for supper. He'd even been treated with a smattering of kindness from her daughters. The food had seemed all right, too, for her flattery had numbed his tastebuds. And in the dark that night she had felt good.

As always, though, the light finally comes. The woman was as obsessed with indoor plumbing as he was with ballet. He could not afford to do the work on her home. That would take time and money away from his presentation. If only he could have told her sooner, but until tonight he always got a knot in his throat and could never say the words. Now he had a knot in his stomach as well.

The goats kept him awake most of the night trying to eat the rag rug right off his body, and so when the first rooster crowed, Xavier, stiff and sore, arose. He had dug in the earth all the day before and bedded on it all night.

It took the sun awhile to climb the other side of the mountains. They seemed flat and black against the rising oranges and yellows, but once the mighty globe shoved its brilliant sabers of light between the peaks, the mountains took form and suddenly the valleys were violet and the hogbacks golden and green.

The chickens scratched around and started visiting. A bird talked somewhere out in the sagebrush. A trailer-truck groaned over a rise on the highway below. A thin blue haze hung over Ragoon from early morning piñon fires. The two curs moved over against the adobe wall where its reflection would give them a double warmth.

Xavier took his morning relief behind the privy, staring at the spot where the money was buried. He had an urge to dig it up but knew that Marion and the daughters would be awake. He was hungry. He headed for his truck, not looking at the house. He walked in an arc to the conveyance as if a pressure exuding from the house had pushed him off a true course.

The old motor choked and spit. Xavier pumped the gas pedal with some hint of desperation, glancing at the house, expecting Marion to crash right through the thick walls and devour him. Finally, the motor, gas and sparks all coordinated and Xavier raced the truck backwards, bumping up on top of a huge clump of sage. He then gunned it in a circle, hit the road hurtling back and forth across it, settled down and rolled on to town.

He had breakfast at a truck stop and went to work. Manuel was there. He was hanging on the pick where it appeared to be stuck in the bottom of the ditch. He had swung at the earth with admirable intent, but the earth had jumped up, meeting his move halfway and jarring his whole body, as sometimes happens when one steps from a curb that is not supposed to be there. For the moment, he was taking no chances on any kind of movement.

Manuel was about three times as long and not a great deal bigger around than the pick. He had spent so many years digging that the instrument was simply an extension of his arms. No matter what his physical discomfort, the visual aspects suggested a very long-armed man leaning comfortably on the world. Xavier's closer inspection of Manuel's face, however, gave the truth away. Sweat was protruding all over his forehead, and his Adam's apple chugged up and down in his throat, necessitating as many swallows to keep the wine down as it had taken to get it there in the first place.

Xavier asked a silly and unnecessary question, as most people seem to do at moments like this, "How you feeling?"

Manuel allowed the question to reverberate through his head a moment until it had time to settle down. "I feel *lack* I been *shoot* at and *mees, sheet* at and *heet*."

Xavier felt he needed no further description of his associate's condition and he entered the house and went to work. In spite of the various forms of turmoil within him he worked harder, faster, and more efficiently than ever. When the Bentlys arrived that afternoon and posed their perpetual question, he could honestly tell them they could move in three days from the present one.

By late afternoon Xavier was so delighted with the fine day's work that he decided to help Manuel in his recovery. They stopped in at the Chico Bar for medicinal purposes only. As the wine was repeatedly served there was a distinct change in Manuel. There was no doubt that he now felt as good or maybe even better than he had the night before. Not only did he do a Mexican hat dance without a hat, but by midnight he was singing 'Guadalajara' and envisioning himself as the Caruso for the entire Spanish world. How the rest of the patrons saw him remains private with them, for all had learned long ago that Manuel's skinny muscles were like those of an eagle. You don't mess around close up with eagles.

Occasionally, certainly not on purpose, Xavier's thoughts

drifted to Marion's home on the hill. He knew she'd be waiting for him. However, these thoughts were fleeting indeed for Chico's place exuded warmth, companionship and safety.

By one o'clock he knew that Manuel was in as good condition as it was possible to attain in that length of time, and so he pondered on his own pleasures and there by the music box he conjured up the great Tamara. My, what a talent! She could even dance to 'Guadalajara.' She whirled and turned and leaped and flew, and smiled at him, then vanished behind the multi-colored music-maker.

The two o'clock closing time came. This did not deter Manuel. He took several bottles of wine and his boss home with him. They sat on the porch out of courtesy to Manuel's wife and seven children. Xavier insisted they must not enter and disturb their sleep. He had not considered that they would probably wake up the entire neighborhood.

They talked of many truths, and spilled a few lies. Xavier told Manuel about the ballet. But Manuel thought it was some kind of Indian corn dance and said many toasts to his red brothers.

". . . and to you, Xavier, my boss, one man who helps makes piss on this earth. Marries gringo womans, and dance with Indians."

Manuel went to sleep on the porch. Xavier took a bottle of wine, crawled sleepily into his truck, and headed home. He drove up just as the sun knocked the shadows out of the sky. He'd been gone exactly twenty-four hours. He was no longer afraid. He knew what he must do and that was it. He'd tell Marion and make her understand. Xavier took another drink of wine just to be sure he wouldn't forget.

XAVIER'S FOLLY

The new sun had slightly blinded him, and it was a moment before his eyes adjusted to the room. It didn't matter that much for the voice was everywhere. It ricocheted from wall to wall, spun in circles, and danced up and down. It whizzed around in his head, kicking his stomach from the inside. A Neanderthal instinct caused him to move around so that the table was between himself and the strongest point of emission. It was fortunate that Marion had no training in baseball, for Xavier would already be dead. Things, heavy things, were zapping through the room along with the voice. It's possible that her aim became faulty because of her movement around the table to get nearer her target. Xavier himself moved to get farther away from the catapult. Fortunately, she was just no good on moving objects.

"Where is the money? The money? You . . . you . . ." She stopped, sputtering, desperately trying to find words that would express her deepest feelings and a weapon that would kill.

Xavier had never been able to say the right things to his wife. In their moments of forced communication such as now he was a total flop. As she hesitated in her fury he stuck the bottle of very cheap wine out in front of him and politely suggested,

"Would you like a little nip?"

Before she could answer he took a large swallow, watching her around the edge of the bottle. This was no time to get careless.

Marion found words again, "Son-of-a-bitch! Son-of-a-bitch! Son-of-a-bitch!"

The daughters were bravely yelling encouragement to

their mother while at the same time wisely staying behind a bolted door.

Xavier, like most honest people, was a poor liar. It comes from a lack of practice. He ventured, "I . . . I lost the money gambling."

"Liar! Liar! You lying bastard!"

He realized that she'd caught on. He had no time to dwell upon it, though, for she now expressed many of those deep feelings she'd been searching for. "I'll have you jailed. I'll sue for the money. I'll sue, you hear?"

Xavier said, "Now, honey . . ." How he came up with that sweet word he could not comprehend.

She went on: "All my life I've had to go outside to the toilet, in blizzards and blazin' sun! It ain't right! You . . . you worthless little pig! You think fixin' a place up is paintin' the toilet door! That's all you've done since we've been married! You didn't even bother to fix the cracks. The wind freezes my ass off in the winter and melts it off in the summer."

Xavier now realized that it was either indoor plumbing or Tamara. No compromise was to be reached. His decision took no struggle at all. He set the bottle down on the table, toward her side. She glared at it, breathing so hard that her drooping breasts actually pushed out momentarily. Her eyes were squinted so that Xavier doubted if she'd ever be able to get them fully open again. There was no use concerning himself about the anger or the disarray of her hair.

She said with meaning, "You son-of-a-bitch."

As always, Xavier spoke the improper words to her even thought he did so with restraint and a certain touch of politeness, "I wish you'd quit calling me by your family name."

That certainly did it. She went right over the table, grabbing the wine bottle on the way. Xavier turned and ran for the door. But now the odds were finally fulfilled. She hurled the bottle and it went straight to its mark, thudding against the back of Xavier's skull just as he was trying to escape through the screen door. He was propelled out and off the porch, face down, in the dirt. The cur dogs were both barking and nipping at him as he stumbled to his feet. The world tipped and rocked, trying to flatten him against its bosom. He could hear the screams behind him and feel the breath of the dogs on his legs. He stayed upright. It wasn't easy either. He managed to fumble his way into the truck and release the brake just as Marion reached out to claw his eyes. But the truck was moving, and as he jerked the door shut it knocked her down. He gave the motor a turn and the saints were kind—it started. He rolled swiftly down the hill and didn't even glance in the rear view mirror.

3

It took nine stitches to sew his head up and the knot throbbed a week, but he and Manuel worked and worked and worked.

Xavier went to see the attorney, Mr. Granger. He smiled at the little plumber, and said,

XAVIER'S FOLLY

"Yes, I was in show business for awhile. It's possible that I could use some of my old connections to find Tamara for you." He made it seem like a very difficult task before he was through. The truth was, Xavier had barely left the office when Granger called a performers' guild in New York and acquired the address of Tamara's agent.

The agent said there was a possibility that in late summer Tamara might have time for a night in Ragoon. It would all be up to the cash offered, availability of proper music, etc., etc. Granger let Xavier wait three weeks before telling him about the ten minutes of calls.

In the meanwhile Xavier rented a very small room in an alley, barely big enough for a cot and all his tools. He ate all his meals right from the cans and had no luxuries. He now worked at night when the houses were new and empty, and by sleeping little and worrying much was accumulating more money all the time. The cache behind Marion's house still had to be recovered, but he simply couldn't bring himself to invade her domain as yet. The new scar on his head still itched.

Marion had told around town that he had attacked her in a drunken rage and she'd fought for her life. She had the law arrest him, but it was only a formality. They quickly observed that she didn't have a scratch on her and Xavier had a nine-stitch hole in his head.

Granger finally received word from Tamara and she could stop over, enroute from Chicago to Los Angeles, the twenty-first day of August, for one night. The cost, Granger said, would be thirty-five hundred and expenses. Actually it was twenty-five, but Granger had to live like anyone else.

He explained to Xavier that at the Met and other large

theatres Tamara worked with a sixty-piece orchestra, and he was having some difficulty convincing them that even though they could only deliver thirty pieces it would be very satisfactory. For a moment this shocked the ecstasy out of Xavier's body, but Granger told him not to worry because he had to make a business trip to Denver soon and he would take care of all the arrangements.

"Strings," exulted Xavier. "Get lots of strings."

Now the word was around town about Xavier's madness and he was greeted with, "How's the impresario today?" "Give my regards to Broadway," and such like.

He rented a small lot in the desert on the opposite side of town from Marion. About thirty yards back from the highway, he started building his stage. Local jokesters called it the 'poor man's Met.' At first the verbal cuts had hurt but now he just worked, and dreamed. He tied on to the power line and when he wasn't plumbing at night he sawed, measured, and gradually nailed his stage together. It would be an outdoor stage with the whole vast southwest as a background. He built a railing for the orchestra. He did Tamara's stage with fine wood, solid and smooth. He put up poles on the corners and in the middle, and strung small ropes crisscrossed over it. On these he hung scores of tiny colored flags.

When the last piece of red cloth was draped, he walked excitedly out into the desert, not looking back till he was on a promontory a good half mile distant. Then he turned; the beauty almost overwhelmed him. It was like a carnival, so gay and joyous. It was alive and breathing. It was his . . . his and Tamara's. The local populace drove by and laughed; strangers stared in wonder at the apparition, but Xavier loved it.

Then Granger called him in for a meeting. It was decided that the cost of attendance would be a flat five dollars. It was now time to have the show cards printed. Xavier had already worked out the design and color. When he took his idea to the newspaper for printing he never dreamed they would do a story on him.

In a few days he got the eighteen by twenty-four inch cards. They were grand—red and yellow with black letters and a photo of Tamara. His name was right next to hers. They read:

XAVIER PRESENTS
The
GREAT TAMARA
Ballerina Supreme

They gave the date, hour and price of admission, as well as the location (as if everyone in the whole of Ragoon County wasn't aware of that). He proudly drove around town putting the cards in every saloon, gas station, and shop. He even put them up in the court house and the county jail. This activity turned almost every individual in town into a comic. Oh, the wise remarks that exist in doubting souls.

Xavier went about building the benches and stringing the lights. He had to import an electrician from the Little Theatre in Albuquerque to install the moving spots. These were covered with pink gel to soften the glow. He kept the man two extra nights just to be sure they were of a proper quality for his Tamara. Yes, she was *his* right now, and forever, no matter what. The electrician would return, for a price, the night of the big DO.

Then the local paper came out with these large letters on the front page: LOCAL PLUMBER TO BE IMPRESARIO???? and the story followed. In spite of the question marks, the local comments of ridicule slowly subsided. They gave glances of fear now, barely smiling. Hadn't the paper actually said the ballerina was coming? What if he really pulled it off? From some of those who had teased the most he now got an occasional, hesitant pat on the back. They were having third and fourth doubts. Everyone fears a winning except other winners.

Marion had received an advance on the land development and had Ben Gonzales up at the house putting in her plumbing. She was so excited about this that she only had time to curse Xavier about one hour out of three. She got a lot of extra work out of Ben by flattering him and stating that he was lucky. Xavier would be broken and shamed out of the county and he'd have the plumbing business all to himself. At this thought she started working on Ben in other ways as she had once done to the little ballet producer. The lady was determined to have her own personal plumber.

Manuel didn't really know what was going on, but with a sense of destiny, he dug deeper, faster and longer, than any man in the history of Ragoon. It was a busy time for plumbers.

4

As mid-August came the town of Ragoon filled up with tourists. Each day hundreds passed through on their way to Colorado, but many stayed. The motels were ninety percent full and the plaza was overflowing with visitors, in varying percentages, from all the states. The Chamber of Commerce and one drug store handled Xavier's tickets. To everyone's amazement except Xavier's, they were sold out by the sixteenth. There were requests for standing room. Many had agreed to bring their own seats and sit in the desert itself.

On the morning of the twentieth, Xavier handed over the needed funds to Granger. The attorney, knowing Xavier's fine earning record, had given checks for the orchestra, etc. Xavier had taken care of all construction, printing, and the like.

Granger raised pencil from paper and said, "Now, that takes care of everything but Tamara and the hotel bill."

Xavier was thanking Granger, "Mr. Granger, I don't know how to . . ."

"Now, now, Xavier. It's all in my duties. Nothing to it. Just glad I could be of help. We're proud of you here in Ragoon." He took on his courtroom voice now, rubbed his prosperous stomach, and continued, "Very proud indeed." And then as an afterthought, "It looks like you're going to have a financial success on your hands as well." And he smiled at Xavier like Santa Claus' great grandfather.

Xavier had several hundred dollars left but he could avoid it no longer, he had to go to Marion's and get his buried

XAVIER'S FOLLY

money. In the adventure, the glow of creating a classic presentation, he'd kept delaying his duty on the hillside until he'd hidden it so far within himself it had actually been forgotten. Well, the dark of night was well suited for digging up money buried ten steps behind the wooden outhouse with a painted door. Even the wise old coyote knew things like this. Xavier had always believed in following nature whenever possible.

Now he would go out and make his last inspection, because tomorrow he would be too busy. The day was warm, the blue grey foothills rolled up merging with the base of the mountains. An aura hung over it all . . . an unseen mist that caused the rays of the sun to break into infinitesimal sundrops exploding in the air with billions of tiny sparkles. The soft sound of a dove cooing caressed the bright air. The bobcat and the coyote rested in the first jumble of rocks, digesting food from last night's hunt, waiting for the moon again. The gophers and the rats were in their dens hiding from the sun. Some of them would not escape the night hunters. Some would. Bugs and lizards crawled under small rocks. The snakes waited in the shade of the sage and cactus and watched their movements. Higher up in the aspen and pine, deer fed, becoming lazy and fat. But at the first explosion of the fall hunter's gun, they would quiver, run and hide, trying to survive. Some wouldn't. But all the movement Xavier could see in this expanse was a hawk circling and the slight stirring of the flags as they made love to a fluctuating breeze. Behind the mountains the clouds rose, shoving up like sails being raised on giant sky ships. Their heaviness turned their bottoms dark with shadow.

The mood of the day, of the time in Xavier's existence,

had caught him up in a reverie of dreams, of glory. Then the first heavy drop of rain hit his shoulder. He looked up. Two more splashed against his face. Then it came down hard, fast, clean and pure. The curtain of moisture moved on over his kingdom and down the hills to the west wetting a path perhaps two thirds of a mile wide.

The freshness of everything was almost more than Xavier could take. What luck! The dust would be perfectly settled for the crowd tomorrow night.

Xavier checked out the ticket sales and the hotel reservations. He called on Granger again to be sure about the orchestra. All was in order. His universe was complete, or would be, after a little trip to the *casa* in the foothills.

At dusk he bought a box of dog biscuits. Then he went to his crowded room and fed himself a can of Vienna sausage, some crackers and an apple. He lay down on the cot to wait. The alarm was set for two o'clock. That would get him at Marion's about three when she would be sleeping the soundest. The girls didn't concern him. They were too lazy to wake up. Sleep avoided Xavier that night. There was too much to think about on the morrow, not counting the risk of facing Marion tonight. He rubbed the scar on his head. The alarm rang, and he quivered all over from shock at the sound.

The moon was almost full. It shoved the blue lights out over the sage and made Xavier wish for total darkness. He thought that the earth's second biggest spotlight was not needed this night. He pulled from the highway, turning off his lights before he did, drove up a little draw and hid the truck. He put on his jacket and emptied the dog biscuits in one large pocket.

XAVIER'S FOLLY

He used the country road for awhile, trying to walk softly. He felt that every step was surely jarring the foundations of the house and rattling dishes in the cupboard. He envisioned Marion sitting cocking the hammers on a brand new shotgun. If she hadn't hated the outdoor privy so, he was sure she'd be waiting there to blow him in half, cursing the undone plumbing while he kicked his last.

Sure enough, when he was within a couple of hundred yards of the house the two dogs ran around barking like never before. Xavier knew they sensed his fear. He jumped off the road behind some sagebrush and held his breath. Xavier *tried* not to *be*—to exist—but he *was*. He was right here cowering while the money resided up there in an unfeeling bucket not caring whether he recovered it or not.

Inside, Marion pushed at Ben Gonzales' sleeping back until he awoke. "There's somethin' out there, Ben."

Now Mr. Gonzales had labored day and night getting her plumbing all in order and had finally finished the task that very evening. He was tired. "Ish jiss a coyote," he mumbled, and went back to sleep.

Xavier moved up to meet the dogs and whatever other demons lurked there for him. He knew now what courage it took for a foot soldier to attack hidden machine guns and cannon. As he neared the dogs, or vice versa, he tried whistling to them with friendship. He really didn't know if he was making a sound or not. Dogs are supposed to feel vibrations beyond the capability of the human ear, and he was not about to exude enough air for Marion's ears.

Now the dogs faced him and they had a combination of irritated barks and disgusted snarls for their former half master. He pitched some biscuits in front of them, whispering love songs as hard as he could.

"Oh, you beautiful dogs. You kind-hearted dogs. You wise and thoughtful dogs. You hungry dogs. Dogs are my friends. Hello, my friends."

It worked somewhat. They did grab up the biscuits greedily. And then stood back with bristles up, growling softly to see what kind of trick or treat was next. Xavier was busy. He made a wide circle to come in behind the outhouse, all the time dropping biscuits to the growling dogs and trying to watch the door to Marion's house. He listened hard, too.

The dogs had decided to adopt the ancient attitude of let's wait and see. They had a growl bottled up just at the end of their tongues ready for instant action if the biscuits were stopped permanently. The jacket pocket was only half full now. Xavier would have to work fast.

And then he saw! The outhouse was gone and all the ground around had been graded smooth! There was Gonzales' work truck. No doubt Gonzales also occupied his late unlamented bed. To save his life, his soul, his presentation, he could not divine the spot where the small structure of relief had stood.

Christ! If he'd just had enough sense to bring along his electronic pipe locator there would be no problem. In a small hysterical moment he thought about borrowing his fellow worker's. It was probably in the back of the truck. However, the truck's proximity to the doorway of Marion's house forbade that.

The dogs were circling now, feeling his anxiety and letting little portions of growls escape. Any moment they might go the whole route. He pitched them two more biscuits, buying time. He thought. Not an easy thing to do either. Watching the door and the dogs he spotted a stick in a pile of wood that had once been the privy. If he remembered correctly the contents of that little building had been somewhat above the level of the earth. That would mean it would be mixed with the soil that covered it.

He made a wild guess as to its location and an even wilder decision. He must become a dog. He threw the rest of the biscuits out around him and dropped down on his hands and knees, punching at the earth, looking for a soft spot, and sniffing back and forth from side to side like a thoroughbred trailhound. At this unusual action the dogs even forgot the biscuits. They growled and let out two rather confused barks.

Marion was not going to accept the coyote theory. This time she kneed Gonzales in the kidneys and forced him up. He stumbled around trying to find the bedroom door.

Suddenly Xavier plunged the stick into soft soil and he got the scent all right. There was no doubt at all. Now he moved back and forth trying to define the edges of the covered hole, sniffing, dropping his head right to the ground to better pin down the outer edges correctly.

Gonzales finally found the door and sort of wobbled through the kitchen and looked out. He tried to rub the sleep from his eyes and then he saw through the blur that there were three dogs in the dimming moonlight. He disgustedly made his way back to the bed and said, "Jish another dog."

Xavier drew the line in the soil and stood up putting his heels on it and took ten steps straight toward a prominent sagebrush. He knelt and scooped the few inches of dirt from his beloved bucket, pulled it out, stood up, looked at the house, then at the dogs. They were doing their growling trick louder now for they realized they had a real thief in their back yard.

Xavier started his circle away from the house, again whispering loving words to the dogs as he went. His steps got faster as they got louder. Then he broke into a run. Now dogs have a great attraction to anything that runs from them, whether it be rabbits, cats, cars or plumbers. They pursued. Loudly. They nipped and circled, making all kinds of exciting noise. Xavier was fending them off fairly well with the bucket. Since he was going downhill and also nearing his means of escape, his speed increased. So did that of the dogs.

Marion sat straight up in bed and suddenly reached over and hit Gonzales on the side of his snoring head. He never did know how he got the sore spot nor why he'd awakened so suddenly.

Xavier made his truck, opened the door, and as he jumped in one of the dogs latched on to his coat tail and the other to his leg. But nothing could stop him now. He kicked them loose and the truck responded to his desire by starting right off and he drove like hell for town as the greatest day of his life announced itself beyond the mountains in the perpetual sky.

5

Granger had volunteered to take his private plane and pick up Tamara and her three associates at the Albuquerque airport. The orchestra was coming in on a chartered bus from Denver. The stage was as ready as it would ever be. Manuel was given the day off and all work stopped. Xavier went to J. C. Penney's and bought a new suit, tie, shirt, socks and even underwear. None of it quite fit, but then creative people are sometimes shoddy in their dress.

The local newspaper carried a half page on the activities and said that representatives of two major T.V. networks would cover the show out of Albuquerque. Everywhere Xavier went he found friends. New friends, old friends, and friends of friends. He just wandered around accepting the attention with smiles and thanks but his mind was on the night. Tonight, yes tonight, he would actually cast his eyes on the moving, living, lovely flesh of Tamara. Had any man in all time ever been so blessed? He said a quiet prayer of thanks. He was so happy and full of wonder that he failed to notice a twenty-mile long column of white clouds peeking constantly higher over the Rocky Mountains.

He checked at the Chamber and the drug store. All tickets were sold. They had even sold out of standing room. The town was full of people and a crowd was gathering in front of the Ragoon Inn. Everyone wanted a glimpse, a touch, a part of the great Tamara.

He worked his way through the crowd to the lobby where he was welcomed by the mayor, the chief of police, the hotel manager, newspaper and T.V. reporters. He was frightened. He was numb. He was in agonized ecstasy. The clicking cameras, flashing lights, and pointed questions, whirled around Xavier in a blurred vortex.

Then he heard the noise and all the flesh moved to the door. He just stood in the lobby and waited. He could not push to see her. It had been too long. It was a long wait of only a minute. His hands perspired and he rubbed them over and over against his coat. He didn't want his right hand wet when he finally touched hers. His feet had melted to the floor. He felt if he took a step part of the hotel rug would pull up and go along with him.

Then he saw Granger smiling, gregariously efficient, leading . . . leading . . . yes, it was Tamara. The lovely Tamara! He saw her dark eyes floating ghostlike through space up to him and he took her hand in both of his and kissed it. That's all he remembered until someone handed him a cup of tea in her suite.

Her wardrobe mistress was busy unpacking. The ballet master and manager was on the phone long distance already planning the next show in another city. One helper held two elegant Afghan hounds on a joined leash and constantly answered the door. With haughty politeness he refused to allow anyone to enter. Granger and the mayor were the only local people present.

Tamara was giving orders on clothing and food for after the show like a true and crowned queen. Xavier was amazed that she was only five feet one and ninety pounds. In her photos she looked six feet tall. In fact, she appeared that now.

Suddenly she turned full on Xavier, asking, "Mr. Del

Campo, could we order you drinks, food, anything? I do neither until after the performance."

He shook his head no, and choked that he would wait too. Then he took a swallow of the tea he had forgotten all about. He couldn't believe he was actually talking with her. They were saying words to each other across the room. They had shared eyes while doing so. She was far more beautiful and graceful than could be imagined. Every move was a poem . . . no, a symphony! Xavier dared not even blink his eyes for fear he'd miss a priceless gesture.

The low distant growl of thunder came to him subconsciously but he ignored its existence. Granger walked and looked out the window towards the mountains. He didn't comment, but gave Xavier a quick glance.

The next hour was a fog to Xavier. He did remember later that she'd commented on the beauty of the land around and how refreshing to perform out of a big city in such clean air.

Outside, and above, the clouds humped over the mountains and spread across the foothills and the valleys. They were dark and solemn like dynamite just before the spark touches. They boiled now and moved together, and the lightning burst out of them, crescendoing sound across the land and shaking the windows of the hotel.

Then there was a pause. A stillness. Tamara, busying herself with her wardrobe, glanced at the window and then at Xavier. Xavier stared into the bottom of his teacup. He was afraid to feel—to know. Then it came, great gushes of water splashing against the panes with its brother wind, running off the walls and joining the little rivulets on the ground. The thunder and lightning became the same sound now, the same entity. So did the beating of Xavier's heart. No one talked for awhile, then Granger and the mayor said they'd call the airport for a weather report and left.

Tamara made light chatter and smiled at Xavier many times. He just sat smiling, with his face. A small smile to be sure, but there, just the same. The storm seemed to talk louder and pound harder.

Suddenly Tamara sent her entourage away. She brought him another cup of tea, and as she bent over he saw the ocean of her eyes. The waves splashed against and over his whole being.

She was at the phone talking. He did not hear. Then the waiter was there, and they sat across a table from each other. There was food he didn't taste, champagne he didn't savor, and talk he didn't hear. But he felt. Had any man *ever* felt all the things he had in the last few seconds, minutes, hours, eternities?

She left him and went to her bedroom, motioning him to wait. Then she came into the room in the dress of the dying swan. She danced. The entire orchestra was down in the bar drinking, but Xavier heard them playing, playing, playing. She floated and flew. Xavier swore to Manuel later that there were whole minutes when she didn't even touch the floor. And then she died. Just for him. Fluttering the life from flesh that had become that of the most graceful of all the world's creatures—the white swan. The bird lay there dead but the lady slowly rose and bowed to him. He clapped so hard his head jarred, and just as his dreams had predicted she came to him, taking his hands, saying,

"Thank you, Señor Del Campo, thank you from the bottom of my soul."

She led him to the door and whispered that it was late. Then she bent slightly and kissed him on the mouth, holding his head in her hands with infinite tenderness. Her eyes spread around him and went with him into the hall, keeping him warm and glowing. It was midnight. He could not go out the front and see anyone. He could not share this moment. It was his alone. He moved to the end of the hall and stepped out onto a fire-escape. He walked down it into the wetness of the same alley he lived on. The rain was over. The eaves still dripped a little. The clouds were spreading apart, making holes for the light of the moon. One beam hit a puddle in front of him. He splashed into the blue mirror.

6

It was never known if anyone drove along the highway at sunup the next morning, but if so, they would have seen the open air stage where the little colored flags hung limp, wet and heavy. A closer examination would have shown a short chunky man standing there looking at his muddy feet. He took two timid steps forward, raised one leg and whirled almost all the way around on the wet wood. And then he smiled.

One-Eyed Sky

1

The cow lifted her muzzle from the muddy water of the tank. She must go now. Her time was at hand. She could feel the pressure of the unborn between her bony hips. With the springless clicking tread of an old, old cow she moved out towards the rolling hills to find a secluded spot for the delivery.

It was late July and the sun seared in at her about an hour high. The moistureless dust turned golden under her tired hoofs as the sun poured soundless beams at each minute particle of the disturbed earth. The calf was late—very late. But this being her eighth and last she was fortunate to have conceived and given birth at all.

The past fall the cowhands had missed her hiding place in the deep brush of the mesas. If found she would have been shipped as a canner, sold at bottom prices and ground into hamburger or Vienna sausage. Not one of the men would have believed she could make the strenuous winter and still produce another good whiteface calf. She had paid the ranch well, this old cow . . . seven calves to her credit. Six of them survived to make the fall market fat and profitable. The coyotes took her first one. But she had learned from that.

She turned from the cowtrail and made her way up a little draw. Instinct guided her now as the pressure mounted in her rear body. It was a good place she found with the grass still thick on the draw and some little oak brush for shade the next sweltering day. The hills mounted gradually on three sides and she would have a down-grade walk the next morning to the water hole. She had not taken her fill of water, feeling the urgency move in her.

She found her spot and the pain came and the solid lump dropped from her. It had not taken long. She got up, licked the calf clean and its eyes came open to see the world just as the sun sank. It would be long hours now before the calf would know other than the night.

It was a fine calf, well boned and strong, good markings. In just a little while she had it on its feet. The strokes of her tongue waved the thick red hair all over. With outspread legs it wobbled a step and fell. She licked some more. Again the calf rose and this time faltered its way to the bag swelled tight with milk.

The initial crisis was over, but as the old cow nudged the calf to a soft spot to bed it down, her head came up and she scented the air. Something was there. As the calf nestled down with its head turned back against its shoulder, the old cow turned, smelling, straining her eyes into the darkness. There was a danger there. Her calf was not yet safe. Nature intended her to eat the afterbirth, but now there would be no chance. She stood deeply tired, turning, watching, waiting.

2

The coyote howled and others answered in some far-distant canyon. It was a still night. The air was desert dry. It made hunting difficult. It takes moisture to carry and hold a scent. Her four pups took up the cry, hungry and anxious to prey into the night.

She, too, was old and this, her fourth litter, suffered because of it. She was not able to hunt as wide or as well as in past years. The ribs pushed through the patched hair on all the pups. They moved about, now and then catching the smell of a cold rabbit trail. Two of the pups spotted prairie mice and leaped upon them as they would a fat fowl, swallowing the rodents in one gulp. It helped, but still they all felt the leanness and the growling of their bellies.

The old coyote turned over a cow chip and let one of the pups eat the black bugs underneath. They could survive this way, but their whole bodies ached for meat.

They moved up to the water hole as all living creatures of the vast area did. The old one had circled carefully, hoping to surprise a rabbit drinking. But there was none. They had already worked the water hole many times before with some success, but now its banks were barren. They took the stale water into themselves to temporarily alter the emptiness.

The old one smelled the tracks of the cow, hesitating, sniffing again. Then she raised her head to taste the air with her nostrils. The pups all stood motionless, heads up, waiting. There was a dim scent there. Not quite clear. The distance was too far, but there was a chance for meat. A small one indeed, but in these hard times the mother could not afford to pass any opportunity. With head dropping now and then to delineate the trail of the old cow, the old coyote moved swiftly, silently followed by four hungry pups copying her every move.

3

Eight miles to the north a cowboy sixty years old, maybe seventy—he had long ago forgotten—scraped the tin dishes, washed them briefly, and crawled in his bunk against the line camp wall. He was stiff and he grunted as he pulled the blanket over his thin eroded body. The night was silent and he thought.

Outside a horse stood in the corral. A saddle hung in a small shed. In the saddle scabbard was a .30-30 for killing varmints. If he had a good day and found no sign of strays in the mighty expanse of the south pasture he could ride on into headquarters the day after next to company of his own kind. It really didn't matter to him so much except the food would be better and the bed a little softer. That was about all he looked forward to now. Tomorrow he, too, would check the water hole for signs. He slept.

ONE-EYED SKY

4

She couldn't see them, but they were there. Their movement was felt and the scent was definite now. She moved about nervously, her stringy muscles taut and every fiber of her being at full strain. When they had come for her firstborn she had fought them well, killing one with a horn in its belly and crippling two more. But finally they had won. The calf—weak as all first calves are—had bled its life into the sand of the gully. She had held the pack off for hours until she knew the calf was dead and then the call from the blood of those to come had led her away to safety. It had been right. All her other calves, and the one resting beside her now, had been strong, healthy.

The scars showed still where they had tried to tear the ligaments from her hocks in that first battle long ago, she had been sore and crippled for weeks. A cowboy had lifted his gun to relieve her misery. But another had intervened. They roped her and threw her to the ground. They spread oil on her wounds and she recovered.

She whirled about, nostrils opening wide from the wind of her lungs. Her horns automatically lowered, but she could see nothing. She was very thirsty and her tongue hung from the side of her mouth. She should have taken on more water, but the enemy would have caught her during the birth and that would have been the end. She would have to be alert now, for her muscles had stiffened with age and the drive and speed she had in her first battle were almost gone. Then too, in the past, many parts of nature, of man and animal enemy had attacked her.

ONE-EYED SKY

In her fourth summer, during a cloudburst when the rains came splashing earthward like a lake turned upside down, a sudden bolt of lightning had split the sky, ripping into a tree and bouncing into her body. She had gone down with one horn split and scorched. Three other cows fell dead near her. For days she carried her head slung to one side and forgot to eat. But she lived.

Later she had gotten pinkeye and the men had poured salt into her eye to burn out the disease.

And she had become angry once while moving with a herd in the fall roundup. She had been tired of these mounted creatures forever crowding her. She kept cutting back to the shelter of the oak brush and finally she turned back for good, raking the shoulder of the mighty horse. The mounted man cursed and grabbed his rope. She tore downhill, heading for the brush, her third calf close at her side. She heard the pounding of the hooves and the whirr of the rope. Deliberately she turned and crashed through a barbed wire fence, ripping a bone-deep cut across her brisket. In that moment the man roped her calf and dismounted to tie its feet. She heard the bawling, whirled, charged at the man. She caught him with her horn just above the knee as he tried to dodge. She whirled to make another pass and drive the horns home. Then another man rode at her and the evil, inescapable snake of a rope sailed from his arm and encircled her neck. Three times he turned off, jerking her up high and then down hard into the earth, tearing her breath from her body until she stood addled and half blind. Then they stretched her out again and turned her loose. She had learned her lesson hard. During the stiff winters and wet spells she limped where the shoulder muscles had been torn apart.

ONE-EYED SKY

But the worst winter of all was when the snow fell two feet deep and crusted over, isolating the herd miles from the ranch house. During the dry summer they had walked twice as far as usual to find the short shriveled grass. She and the others had gone into the winter weak and their bellies dragged in the drifts. When they tried to walk on top of the white desert the crust broke and they went down struggling, breathing snow and cold into their lungs, sapping their small strength. The icy crust cut their feet and they left red streaks in the whiteness. And the wind came driving through their long hair, coating their eyes and nostrils with ice. They'd wandered blindly, piling into deep drifts, perishing.

Finally the wagons—pulled by those same horses she had hated so much—broke through the snow. They tailed her up and braced her and got some hay into her mouth. Once more she survived.

The old cow had a past and it showed in her ragged, bony, tired, bent, scarred body. And it showed in her ever-weakening neck as the head dropped a fraction lower each time she shook her defiance at the night and the unseen enemy.

The moon came now and caressed the land with pale blueness. It was like a single, headless, phosphorescent eye staring at the earth seeing all, acknowledging nothing. The moon made shadows and into these she stared and it would seem to move and then she would ready herself for the attack. But it didn't come. Why did they wait?

The night was long and the moon seemed to hang for a week, then the sun moved up to the edge of the world chasing the moon away.

ONE-EYED SKY

Her tongue was pushed out further now and her eyes were glazed, but she stood and turned and kept her guard. She saw the old, mangy coyote directly down the draw facing her, sitting up on its haunches panting, grinning, waiting. It took her awhile to see the pups. They were spotted about the hills, surrounding her. But these did not worry her. They would not move until the old one did. Nevertheless she cast her dimming eyes at them, letting them know she knew—letting them know she was ready.

The calf stirred and raised its head and found the glorious world. First it must feed. She moved swiftly to it, watching the old coyote as she did so. The new one struggled up, finding its way to the teat. The cow saw the muscles tense all over the old coyote. Its head tilted forward as did its pointed ears. Then it moved from side to side, inching closer at each turn. The pups got to their feet, ready for the signal. But it didn't come. The old coyote retreated. It was a war of nerves. And because the coyote fights and dies in silence, when the time arrived there would be no signal visible to the cow, only to the pups.

Now the calf wanted to explore. It wanted to know into what it had been born. Already the color and the form of plant and rock and sky were things of wonder. There was so much to see and so little time for it. Again the mother bedded down her calf—a heifer it was—and soon the warm air and full stomach comforted it.

By midmorning the coyote had faked ten charges. And ten times the cow had braced to take the old one first and receive and bear the rear and flanking attacks until she could turn and give contest. She knew from the past they would all hit her at once, diving, feinting, tearing from all sides.

But if she could keep the calf from being mortally wounded until she disposed of the old one they had a chance. But with each rise in temperature, with each drying, burning moment of the sun without water, her chances lessened.

By noon the heat was almost blinding her. She felt the trembling and faltering in her legs. All the old wounds were making themselves known now and her tongue hung down, parched and beginning to swell. Her breathing came hard and heavy. The nostrils caked from the powdered dirt of her restlessness and her eyes filled around the edges and watered incessantly. But the coyote waited. And so did the old cow. Life had always been a matter of waiting—waiting for the calf each year, waiting for the greenness of spring, waiting for the wind to die and the cold to quit and the snow to melt. But, win or lose, she would never see another spring. They would find her this fall and ship her away to the slaughterhouse. And if they didn't, the winter, the inexorable winter winds, would drive through her old bones and finish her. But now she had a chore, a life-and-death chore for sure. She would do her natural best.

In the middle of the afternoon she imagined she could smell the water, so near and yet so far away. She bawled out of her nearly closed throat and the tongue was black, and down the other side of her mouth thick cottonlike strings of saliva hung and evaporated in the interminable heat. Her legs had gradually spread apart and she wove from side to side, taking all her strength now just to stand. And right in the pathway to the water sat the laughing coyote beginning to move back and forth again, closer. Closer. As the sun moved lower and lower, so the coyote came nearer, lying down, looking straight at her.

The coyote lay very still, nothing moving but the pink tongue. Yellow eyes watching, glowing like suns. Ten minutes. Twenty minutes. The coyote came from the ground without warning, straight in and fast. The cow knew the others were coming too. She braced herself.

5

The mother coyote followed the trail into scent range of the old cow. Her nostrils told her of the new one. Cautiously she moved up now, almost like a cat. The young tried mightily to do as well. It was no use. The quick, intense movement of the cow revealed her knowledge of their presence. They would have to wait. Methodically she went about spotting her young. She ringed the old cow in, giving soundless directions to her pups to stay put.

The scent of birth, the calf, the old cow brought taste glands into action. The natural impulse was to attack as their stomachs drew narrow and craving. But the coyote could tell from the alertness of the old cow that an early assault would be sure death to some. The hours would be long but the cow would weaken. Much of the moisture had been drained from her body in the birth. The sun would be their ally. They could have the early luxurious feast of the tender veal, and the lean meat of the old cow would last for days—even with the vultures and the magpies to contend with. She could fatten and strengthen the pups and make them ready for mating as her mother had done her. Yes, her mother had been a good teacher and she had learned well. She had been taught to hunt under rotten logs, cow chips and anthills for insects in case of hard times. The field mouse had often saved her from starvation. The lowly grasshopper had filled her belly many times and given her strength to catch larger, tastier game. She learned to steal into a hen yard, make a quick dash, throttling the fowl and escaping before the rancher could get his guns. All of these things she had taught or was teaching her own. But now must come the ultimate lesson—how to down and kill an animal weighing as much as fifteen of their own kind. Besides, they were desperate in their near-starvation.

The old coyote took the main chance in locating herself in the path of the water hole. This was the weak point and she must handle it with care, cunning and courage. She could not fail, for they too would weaken in the long vigil.

She carried a .30-30 slug in her belly from the past. She only felt it on cold or hungry nights. Her tail was shortened and ugly at the end. Her ear was split and torn. A scar ran across her back. One foot was minus two toes.

The ear and tail wounds had come about at the same time. She had learned a hard lesson from this action. She was almost grown then and hunted with the rest of the litter. They had stopped behind a clump of bear-grass, watching the pickup truck circle slowly. They had seen these things before, but no danger had threatened. Suddenly the thing stopped. From its back dropped six large, running hounds. Two teams.

The coyotes moved out too late. Instinct split them in three directions. But the hounds had their speed, and in less than a quarter of a mile each team had downed one of the brood. She alone escaped. On a little rise she whirled watching the hounds bear down on her brother and sister, crushing the life away with their awful fanged jaws. She sailed down from the hill and at full speed crashed into the nearest team, knocking them loose and giving her brother a chance to rise. But it didn't work. Two of the hounds flung the wounded one against the earth again. The third gave chase. She strained away in terror, knowing she could not compete with its size and strength. The hound reached for her throat but missed her and ripped the ear apart instead. They both rolled in a choking spurt of dust. As she rose, the hound clamped her tail. She broke free leaving a humiliating part of herself in his jaws. The chase was more uphill now, and she learned that hounds slowed on that sort of run and never again was she caught on the level or going downhill. She escaped. Alive. Wiser. Alone.

She learned to respect the metallic wheeled things for another reason. She had watched one from a safe distance, as far as hounds were concerned, and suddenly a black something stuck from it and then something struck her in the belly, knocking her over and down. It had been close. She bled badly inside and by the time the bleeding clotted she was very weak from hunger. All that saved her was the finding of a wounded antelope dragging itself into the tall grass of the prairie to die. But now she could smell a gun from a considerable distance. They would not hurt her again in this manner.

Her first sister had eaten poison and died before her eyes. They would not slay her in this vile way, either.

The scar on her back had come from one of those men

who whirl the rope and ride horses. She was looking in a sheep pasture for a lamb to carry to her first litter of pups. She was so intent on her job she did not see the cowboy coming through the gate some half mile distant. But as he neared she felt him even before she cast her glance back over her shoulder. He came on full speed on a fast quarterhorse, whirling the rope. She did not know what it was, but she felt its danger as she did that of a gun. He was upon her and she heard the whirr of the rope mingled with the ground-jarring thump of hooves. She hit the manywired sheep fence without slacking speed. She went through, tearing her back on the vicious barbs. Her neck was sore and twisted for many days. But she lived to hunt again.

The worst of all were the steel jaws the men put in the earth. Once, when she had been hungry, the scent of hog cracklings, and also the urine of one of her own, came to her. Bait. This gave her the confidence to inspect even though the faint scent of man was intermingled. The jaws had grabbed her as she vainly leaped away. She struck the end of the chain where it ran up out of the ground and tightened between the trap and the heavy rock that anchored it. She fought wildly and in great pain for a while, gnawing at her foot until exhaustion stilled her violent action.

She studied the rusty, hard, impersonal steel. It had her. But if she was to die she would do it on the mesa—her home. Foot by painful foot, yard by wrenching yard, she dragged the rock. The man had intended her to hang the trap in some brush flexible enough to keep from tearing the foot loose. It hung, all right, hundreds of times, but never for long.

It took her two days to get to the edge of the mesa. The

foot was swollen almost to the knee joint now and her yellow eyes were red from suffering. Then the stone hung between a crack in the rocks. She fell off the other side and rolled down the rough boulders. The trap and a part of her foot remained in the rocks.

She lived again, less able than before.

Under the recent rising of the staring moon the coyote studied the old cow. It was obvious she was weakening. Soon she would lie down and then . . . but the old cow stood and at the break of day she suckled her young, looking straight at the coyote and shaking her head in answer to the coyote's slavering jaws. The coyote moved in now, taunting, teasing, draining another ounce of strength from the old cow.

The sun came soon, hot and red, striking the old cow in the side of her head. The pups squatted and waited with hunger pounding at their every nerve.

By midday the old coyote could feel the muscles trembling and jerking with weakness in her forelegs and the stomach walls seemed glued together, devouring themselves. She now badly needed water and food. At times the earth diffused into the molten rays of the sun and it looked as if the cow had dissolved. At other moments she bunched her muscles imagining the cow attacking. She sat with her tongue out and an eternal laughing expression in all her face except the eyes. They seared through the sun's rays, hungrily, with a quiet desperation and sureness.

The old cow's head was dropping now. She was slipping fast. But still she stood and every time the coyote moved in her snake-track advance the cow raised her head a little and tossed the pointed swords.

ONE-EYED SKY

There was no backing out now. No changing of plans. The old mother coyote and her brood would soon be so weakened they would surely fall prey to one of their many worldly enemies. Survival now meant the death of the old cow.

The coyote drew in its dry tongue and dropped it again into the dry air and waited. The sun moved on and the old cow's legs spread a little more. The coyote could see her weaving and straining to stay upright. The tender, living veal of the calf lay folded up beside her.

Now the time was present. She sent her message of alertness to her pups. They stood ready, watching, muscles bunched, hearts pounding above the strain of hunger, thirst and heat. She moved forward and lay down to deceive the old cow. Motionless she waited and waited more. All of her being cried to lunge forward, but still she waited. She had decided on the cow's muzzle. She would dart in between the horns, locking her fangs in their breathing softness, and hang on until the aid of her pups downed the old cow. Then? It would be over shortly. A bit torn here and there and the loss of blood would finish her. Then the feast.

The burning eyes of the old coyote and the old cow were fixed on each other now. They both knew what they must do. The old coyote sent the unseen, unmoving signal to her pups and she came from the ground at the same instant, aiming straight and swift between the horns of the old cow.

6

The man arose from the bunk as stiffly as he had crawled into it. It was not quite daybreak. He clothed himself and pulled hard to get his boots on. He built a fire in the squatty iron stove and put the coffeepot on. Then he washed his face and hands in cold water. He placed a skillet on the stove by the coffeepot. Methodically he sliced thick chunks of bacon from the hog side. He took the last of the sourdough batter, tore small balls from it, placing them in a dutch oven on the stove. This done he rolled a smoke, coughing after the first puff. Soon he had a large tin cup of scalding coffee. Another cigarette, another cup. Then he ate. He wiped up the syrup on his plate with his bread. He washed the utensils and put them back on the shelf. He, or someone else, would be here another time. He went out to the corral.

If he was lucky this day and found no strays he could head for the main ranch house tomorrow morning, or if the moon was good he might ride on in tonight. He had two horses here. One ran in a small horse trap adjoining the corrals. The other he had kept up for the ride today.

He brushed his horse's back with his hand and under his belly where the cinches would fit to be sure nothing was lodged in the hair that would cut or stick. He bridled and saddled, put on his chaps and spurs and led the horse up a few steps before mounting. He rode him around the corral several times to limber him up. Then he dismounted, opened the gate, got back on, and rode south just as the sun was melting the night.

ONE-EYED SKY

It was eight miles in a beeline to the water hole. If there were a stray in the huge pasture it would be nearby. He would probably have a twelve-mile ride, what with checking out the sign in the draw and gullies.

The sun was up now, hot for so early in the morning. It was the kind of day that made all living creatures seek shade. Well, he had always wanted a little place with lots of shade trees and water. Especially water. It wouldn't matter how big it was if there was just plenty of water. He would never forget the drought that had sent his family to the final sheriff's sale and moved them from their ranch into a tent on the edge of the little western town to take other folks' laundry, charity, handouts. His pa had already loaned him out to local ranchers. So, he just took a steady job with one of them. At first he worked only for his board and blanket. He gardened, he milked, he shoveled manure out of barns. He patched roofs. He rebuilt corrals. He chopped a whole year's supply of firewood. He ran rabbits in holes and twisted them out with the split end of a barbwire.

And then the drought was over and the grass and cattle came back to the land. He was promoted to horse wrangler which only meant one more chore. He was up before anyone in the morning riding into the horse pasture, bringing in the day's mounts for the cowboys. But things finally got better. His boss saw him top out a waspy bronc and he was allowed to ride with the men. He got five dollars a month and felt proud. Mighty proud. He learned the ways of the range and the handling of cattle and horses. And at the age of seventeen he could draw down twenty dollars a month with room and board. By the time he had worked on ten or twelve different outfits and reached the age of twenty-five he could demand and get thirty dollars a month. Things weren't all bad.

Then a fellow cowboy with a talent for talk convinced him they were in the wrong business.

"Now look here, Snake" (that was his name at the time from being bitten by a rattlesnake), "we're makin' thirty dollars a month, right?"

"Yeah."

"Well, how much you figure a broke-out saddle horse would bring?"

"Oh, round thirty, forty dollars."

"There you are. Now, if a man could ride out say eight or ten a month?"

"I'll have to get a pencil. Besides where you goin' to get that many horses and how much you got to give for them?"

"That's just the deal. Up north in the rough country there's hundreds of wild horses. Now, I had some experience at catching them boogers when I was a kid. We're crazier than hell stayin' around here when we can get rich on our own."

So, he took all he had, two hundred and ten dollars, two head of saddle horses, one saddle, four used ropes and moved north with the talkin' cowboy. The money went fast. It was used to buy packmules and supplies.

They pitched camp and started riding the hills and canyons for sign. The horses were there, all right. But a man could ride all day and never actually see anything but tracks. They were wilder than deer by a whole lot. So the two cowboys set to work building brush corral traps in the narrow part of some canyons on the trail to the watering places. Then they built a round pole corral near camp to break the horses out. It took some wild reckless riding to pen these animals but pen some of them they did. Then they found the horses fought like bobcats and it took some doing just to get a rope on one and snub him up. It was impossible to drive them, so they tied a twisted rawhide garter on one leg. The circulation was cut off and the leg became numb and useless. It wasn't so hard to handle them then.

That was only the beginning of their troubles. When they castrated the studs, half of them died. Most of the rest lost their spirit and became dead-headed and listless.

After a good try they drifted out of the rough country ahead of the winter snow. They had two half-broken mares. But it beat walking because without them that's exactly what they would be doing. Well, they went back—at thirty a month—to the cow-punching job they had left. He started saving again. Finally a rancher offered him a foreman's job at thirty-five a month and he could run as many head of his own cattle as he could acquire.

After a few months, when he had some cash to go on, he made his move. He began trading with the Mexicans. A few dollars down, a worn-out saddle, an old rifle and so on were his barter goods. In three years he had built his herd up to sixty head of cows, twelve steers and two bulls. They were a mixed lot and they were his, but the land they ranged on was not. He still couldn't figure why his boss had been so generous. Another thing he couldn't figure out was why the owner and two of his hands did so much riding without him. He didn't ask questions because it looked like a man would be a fool to tinker with good times. They were mighty scarce.

His boss sent him to a roundup over west at a neighboring ranch. His job was to check out any of their strays and deliver them back to the home range. It was a big outfit and the roundup went on for several days. The last of the work was done right at headquarters. The cowboys ate at the cookhouse. There was a pretty little brown-headed girl doing the cooking. Fine tasty chuck it was. She was the owner's daughter, Nelda.

Well, he kept eyeballing her and she kept glancing back. He was pretty good-looking at that time . . . in a rough, healed-over way. The aging and scars of the tough life hadn't taken hold yet. On the last day before he started home with his gather he asked her for a date, and he damn near fainted when she accepted.

He borrowed a buggy and picked her up late Saturday afternoon. They went to a dance at the schoolhouse. She was all decked out in a long, flimsy, turquoise dress that hugged her up close around the waist and bosom. Her hair just sparkled like her brown eyes and that was like a fall sun striking new frost on a golden aspen leaf. He was so scared and so cockeyed proud that he danced every set with her, even though he had a heck of a time fending off the other cowboys.

About four o'clock in the morning a little before daybreak when the music was slow, he walked outside and leaned her up against the building. While the coyotes howled out in the prairie he pulled her up hard and said: "I . . . I love you. I sure do."

Although she didn't say anything she let him know how she felt with her arms and her eyes. Sweet.

They went steady then. His luck just kept running. He

got into a poker game with a bunch of mining and timber men and won six thousand dollars. That was more money than he had seen all his life put together. He couldn't wait to get over and tell Nelda.

They rode together in the hills and he loved her and she loved him. He told her about the money and how it was not only burning a hole in his pocket but was burning right smack through his leg.

"Snake," she said, "you've got a good start on a herd and the Larking place is for sale. We wouldn't owe more than eighteen thousand."

Eighteen thousand dollars! It scared him. It was beyond him. He would never make it. He just couldn't take on a woman like her, the daughter of a big rancher, owing that kind of money.

Well, he got drunk in town and didn't show up for work. The boss fired him and told him to come and get his cows, at the same time he said there would be no hurry about it. Somehow it didn't make sense.

Snake stayed in town that fall and on into the winter trying to make up his mind what to do. In the meantime the money was going steadily out for whiskey and gambling.

The winter came and a blizzard hit. Most of his cattle walked off into deep drifts of snow and froze to death. By the time he sobered up it was spring and he was broke.

Then the law came and took him. His ex-boss was right there shaking his head and saying he couldn't believe it, after all he had done for him. They railroaded him and now he knew that he had been a blind and a cover-up for the rancher's thievery. He got a year and a day. After three dreary months inside the prison wall he planned to kill the man who sent him there, but then they put him out on the prison farm and he reasoned it wasn't worth it.

He didn't return to the home country for a long time after his release. Nelda married someone else and he kind of regretted he had been so undecided.

He tried a lot of things after that, plunging hard to come back—prospecting, timber leasing, nothing worked out. He was trying to keep from going back to punching cows. He took a job as a dude wrangler in Yellowstone Park. His natural friendliness, his knowledge of horses and everything attracted a lot of business. He had several chances to marry rich widows and cowboy-smitten girls. But he never could decide when the time came. He had heard that all was not roses and sweet violets with the rich dames. A man had to go around with his hand out all the time.

At last, though, he chose to take on this woman from St. Louis. She had come right out and told him she would buy and pay for a ranch, stock it in his name and put some money in the bank in the same manner.

Then he got drunk in Pony, Montana, on bootleg whiskey. It poisoned him and he was laid up out of his head for sixty days. The doctors almost gave up on him. By the time he came to and acquired strength enough to walk and talk, the widow had disappeared. The wrangler who had taken his job ran off to Mexico with her. If only a man could ever make up his mind at the right time he would have this world singing *his* songs he figured.

He kept trying and bumming around into one thing and another. He damned near starved. The years were beginning to show. Finally he returned to his old country and the only thing he really knew—punching cows. The wages were one hundred and twenty-five dollars a month and board. That was tops, as high as he could go in his profession. It was a job that took guts, natural skill, and understanding of the earth and its animals, both wild and domestic, though the present wages wouldn't buy as much as twenty dollars had in his youth. But there he was now riding the draws around the water hole looking for sign and finding none.

It was midafternoon and hot. If he turned back now he could make it in a little after dark, saddle a fresh horse and go on into headquarters. It was three days till payday. He could take his check, go into town, buy a new pair of jeans, a new rope, maybe a new hat. If he was careful he might have enough left over to get a little drunk and maybe even play a little poker. He really needed a pair of new boots but anything worth working in cost between forty and fifty dollars so he would just have to wait till next payday —or the next.

He decided to go on and check the water hole just in case he had missed something. It would cost him another night in the line camp but, after all, what was one more night alone to him? He saw the usual sign of wildlife and was surprised to find the day-old tracks of a cow. One lonely cow. She must have strayed in here to calve, he thought. He could tell by the way her hooves splayed out and by the withered cracks around the edges that she was an old cow.

As he followed her tracks up the trail he noticed that a coyote and four pups had been ahead of him. Probably went right on, he thought, and then an uneasiness came over him. Man, it was hot. He pulled his hat back and wiped the sweat from his forehead and out of his narrow sun-washed eyes. The cow had turned off across a small ridge and he saw the tracks of the coyotes do the same. Pretty soon he felt the horse bunch under him. The head came up and the ears pitched forward. He thought he heard a sound, a cow bawling maybe, but he wasn't sure. He got down and tied the horse to a bush.

He removed the .30-30 from the scabbard and started easing forward. He was slow in his movement because of the stiffness from the long day in the saddle and many years of breaks and bruises. Then he was on his belly crawling forward feeling an excitement that he couldn't define. It was more than the hunter's blood surging now.

He raised up carefully from the side of a yucca plant. He saw the old cow first and then, slowly, one at a time, he located the coyotes. They hadn't seen or heard him yet because of the dryness and lack of wind.

He eased the rifle and sighted down it at the old mother coyote as she moved forward. Just as he started to pull the trigger she lay down right out in front of the old cow. For some reason strange to him he held his fire.

7

In the little hollow where the man, the coyotes, the cow and her calf lay there was concentrated the most life for miles in every direction. Five miles to the north and west in the cedar- and piñon-covered hills twenty-six buzzards circled and lighted on the remains of a cow downed two days before by a mountain lion that lay now in the coolness of the rocks with a full belly; to the east another pack of coyotes was desperately stalking a herd of swift antelope with no luck at all.

A hawk circled curiously above the draw with the man and the animals, smelling meat. The land itself was covered sparsely with buffalo and grama grass and, everywhere, the yucca plants bayonetted the sky. Now and then in meandering, meaningless lines, the land was cut by wind and water erosion forming a rolling, twisted terrain that on the face of a man would have portrayed deep torment.

The man felt the trigger of the rifle with his finger. The hammer was thumbed back. His cheek lay hot and sweating along the stock. The sights were centered on the thin rib cage of the coyote lying so very still. He could tell by the torn, powdered earth around the old cow, standing, swaying so weakly with far-drooped head, that she had held them at bay a long number of hours now.

His eyes raised again and counted the pups. One shot would do it. He must have killed two or three hundred of these animals, these varmints, these predators. He was a good shot. He would not miss. His eyes were in the second sight that comes briefly to older men. He could see almost as good as he could at twenty-one. His stomach was hollow. And he thought vaguely that it had been many hours since he had eaten or drunk. It came to him then that the creatures before him had been much longer without repast.

A sudden admiration came over him for the old, hungry, thirsty coyote and the old, hungry, thirsty cow eying each other in the golden blazing, dying sun. His duty, his real job, was to kill the old coyote and as many of her young as possible and drive the old cow to water, carrying the calf across the swells of his saddle for her. In a day or two she would have her strength back, then he could drive her on to the main herd. That was his job. But he didn't move and all of his long life came to him now as he studied what he saw before him.

The old coyote knew what she must do and she was doing it with every particle of cunning, courage and instinct in her emaciated body. Her pups must be fed and she must, too, if she was to survive and finish their training.

And the old cow had long ago reconciled herself to her fate. She would stand and fight—win or die.

The indecision was not theirs. This trait was his and had always been so.

Time became a vacuum in the floating dust. The bawling of the old cow, just a whisper now, came to him. The coyote lay like dry wood. The pups watched her, their bodies slowly evaporating in the ceaseless sun. It was everything.

His lungs ached from the shallow breathing, but still he could not move the finger that fraction of an inch that would end it. Time. Timeless time.

Then the old coyote attacked as if hurled from the earth. The pups charged down. The man fired but the bullet struck into the shoulder of one of the pups instead. The momentum carried it forward and down and over. It kicked its life away. He raised the gun and fired again. The hindquarters of another pup dropped. He levered another shell and shot it though the head.

As the old coyote came in, lips peeled back, fangs sharp and anxious, the old cow pulled a tiny ounce of strength

ONE-EYED SKY

from her heart—a little reserve she had saved for her young. She shuffled forward to meet the terrible threat.

The sound of the shot had caused the old coyote to veer just a fraction at the last thrust, and it was just enough. The lightning-splintered horn of the old cow drove between the lean ribs and she made one upward swing of her head. The horn tore into the lungs and burst the arteries of the chest apart. The coyote hung there. The cow could not raise her head again. She fell forward crushing at the earth. When she pulled her head and horns away the coyote blinked her yellow, dying eyes just once. It was over.

The other two pups ran out through the brush. They were on their own now.

The calf got to its feet and sucked a little milk from the mother's flabby bag. The man went back to his horse wondering why he had shot the pups instead of the old one. For a moment he had known. But now the knowledge was gone.

In a little while as the sun buried itself in the great ocean of space behind the earth the old cow, her calf at her side, stumbled downhill to water.

Candles in the Bottom of the Pool

1

Joshua Stone III moved along the cool adobe corridor listening to the massive walls. They were over three feet thick, the mud and straw solidified hard as granite. He appeared the same.

The sounds came to him faintly at first, then stronger. He leaned against the smooth dirt plaster and heard the clanking of armor, the twanging of bows, the screams of falling men and horses. His chest rose as his lungs pumped the excited blood. His powerful hands were grabbing their own flesh at his sides. It was real. Then the struggles of the olive conquerors and the brown vanquished faded away like a weak wind.

He opened his eyes, relaxing slightly, and stepped back, staring intently at the wall. Where was she? Would she still come to him smiling, waiting, wanting? Maybe. There was silence now. Even the singing of the desert birds outside could not penetrate the mighty walls.

Then he heard the other song. The words were unintelligible, ancient, from forever back, back, back, but he felt and understood their meaning. She appeared from the unfathomable reaches of the wall, undulating like a black wisp ripped from a tornado cloud. She was whole now. Her black lace dress clung to her body, emphasizing the delicious smoothness of her face and hands. The comb of Spanish silver glistened like a halo in her hair. His blue eyes stared at her dark ones across the centuries. They knew. She smiled with much warmth, and more. One hand beckoned for him to come. He smiled back, whispering,

"Soon. Very soon."

"YES, YES, YES," she said and the words vibrated about, over, through, under and around everything. He stood, still staring, but there was only the dry mud now.

He turned, as yet entranced, then shook it off and entered through the heavily timbered archway into the main room. The light shafted in from the patio windows illuminating the big room not unlike a cathedral. In a way it was. Santos and bultos were all over. The darkly stained furniture was from another time, hand hewn and permanent like the house itself.

He absorbed the room for a moment, his eyes caressing the old Indian pots spotted about, the rich color of the paintings from Spain, the cochineal rugs dyed from kermes bugs. Yes, the house was old; older than America. He truly loved its feeling of history, glory and power.

Then his gaze stopped on the only discord in the room. It was a wildly colored, exaggerated painting of himself. He didn't like the idea of his portrait hanging there. He

CANDLES IN THE BOTTOM OF THE POOL

didn't need that. He allowed it only because his niece, Aleta, had done it. He was fond of her.

Juanita, the aged servant, entered with a tray. It held guacamole salad, tostados and the inevitable bloody Marys. He asked her in perfect Spanish where his wife Carole was.

She answered in English, "On the patio, Señor. I have your drinks." She moved out ahead of him, bony, stiff, bent but with an almost girlish quickness about her. She'd been with them for decades. They'd expected her demise for years, then given up.

Carole lounged in the desert sun, dozing the liquor away. He couldn't remember when she started drinking so heavily. He had to admit that she had a tough constitution—almost as much as his own. It was usually around midnight before alcohol dulled her to retire. She removed the oversized sun glasses and sat up as Juanita placed the tray on a small table by her. The wrinkles showed around the eyes, but her figure was still as good as ever. She rubbed at the lotion on her golden legs and then reached for her drink. At her movement he had a fleeting desire to take her to bed. Was that what had brought them together? Was that what had held them until it was too late? Maybe. She pushed the burnt blonde hair back and placed the edge of the glass against her glistening lips. He thought the red drink was going down her throat like weak blood to give her strength for the day. He gazed out across the green mass of trees, grass, and bushes in the formal garden beyond the patio. He heard the little brook that coursed through it giving life to the oasis just as the bloody Marys did his wife.

It was late morning and already the clouds puffed up beyond the parched mountains, promising much, seldom giving. It was as if the desert of cacti, lizards, scorpions and coyotes between the mountains and the hacienda was too forbidding to pass over. It took many clouds to give the necessary courage to one another. It rarely happened.

He picked up his drink, hypnotized by the rising heat waves of the harsh land.

"I've decided," he said.

"You've decided what?"

"It's time we held the gathering."

She took another sip, set it down and reached for a cigarette. "You've been talking about that for three years, Joshua."

"I know, but I've made up my mind."

"When?"

"Now."

"Now? Oh God, it'll take days to prepare." She took another swallow of the red drink. "I'm just not up to it. Besides, Lana and Joseph are in Bermuda. Sheila and Ralph are in Honolulu."

"They'll come."

"You can't just order people away from their vacations." She took another swallow, pulled the bra of her bikini up, walked over and sat down on the edge of the pool and dangled her feet in it. Resentment showed in her back. He still felt a little love for her, which surprised him. There was no question that his money and power had been part of her attraction to him. But at first it had been good. They'd gone just about everywhere in the world together. The fun, the laughs, the adventure had been there even though some part of his business empire was always intruding. What had happened? Hell, why didn't he admit it? Why didn't she? It had worn out. It was that simple.

Just plain worn out from the heaviness of the burdens of empire like an old draft horse or a tired underground coal miner.

She splashed the water over her body, knowing from his silence there was no use. "Well, we might as well get on with it. When do you call?"

He finished the drink, stood up, and moved towards the house, saying, "As I said, now."

2

Joshua entered the study. His secretary for the past ten years looked up, sensing something in his determined movement.

"All right, Charlotte."

She picked up the pad without questioning. He paced across the Navajo rugs, giving her a long list of names. Occasionally he'd run his hands down a row of books, playing them like an accordian. He really didn't like organization, but when he decided, he could be almost magical at it. There was no hesitation, no lost thought or confusion. He was putting together the 'gathering' just as he'd expanded the small fortune his father had left him. It kept growing, moving.

When he finished dictating the names, he said, "We'll have food indigenous to the southwest. Tons of it. I want for entertainment the Russian dancer from Los Angeles,'

Alfredo and his guitar from Juarez, the belly dancer what's-her-name from San Francisco, the Mariachis from Mexico City, and the brass group from Denver."

His whole huge body was vibrating now. A force exuded from Joshua—the same force that had swayed decisions on many oilfield deals, land developments, cattle domains and on occasion even the stock market—but never had Charlotte seen him as he was now. There was something more, something she could not explain. Then he was done. He pushed at his slightly greying mass of hair and walked around the hand-carved desk to her. He pulled her head over to him and held it a moment against his side. They had once been lovers, but when she came to work for him that was over. There was still a tenderness between them. She was one of those women who just missed being beautiful all the way around, but she had a sensual appeal and a soft strength that was so much more. She had his respect, too, and that was very hard for him to give.

He broke the mood with, "Call Aleta and Rob first."

She took the book of numbers and swiftly dialed, asking, "Are you sure they're in El Paso?"

"Yes. Aleta's painting. She's getting ready for her show in Dallas." He took the phone, "Rob, is Aleta there?"

In El Paso, Rob gave an affirmative answer and put his hand over the phone: "Your Uncle *God* is on the horn."

Aleta wiped the paint from her hands and reached for the receiver. "Don't be so sarcastic, darling; he might leave you out of his will."

The vibrations were instantaneous down the wire between the man and the girl. She would be delighted to come.

When the conversation was over and Aleta informed her

husband, he said, "The old bastard! He's a dictator. I'd just love to kill him!"

He finished with Lana and Joseph Helstrom in the Bahamas with, "No kids. Do you understand? This is not for children."

The husband turned to wife, saying, "We're ordered to attend a gathering at Aqua Dulce."

"A gathering?"

"A party. You know how he is about labeling things."

"Oh Christ, two days on vacation and he orders us to a party."

"I could happily murder the son of a bitch and laugh for years," Joseph said, throwing a beach towel across the room against a bamboo curtain.

Finally Joshua was finished. Charlotte got up and mixed them a scotch on the rocks from the concealed bar behind the desk. They raised their glasses and both said at the same time,

"To the gathering." They laughed together as they worked together.

Suddenly Charlotte set her glass down and, not having heard the phone conversations, stated almost omnipotently, "Half of them would delight in doing away with you."

Joshua nodded, smiling lightly. "You're wrong, love, a good two thirds would gladly blow me apart and all but a few of the others would wish them well."

"Touché."

"They do have a tendency to forget how they arrived at their present positions. However, that's not what concerns me. All are free to leave whenever they wish, but most don't have the guts. They like cinches but never acknowledge that on this earth no such thing exists. Even the sun is slowly burning itself to death."

"Another drink?"

"Of course. This is a moment for great celebration."

She poured the drinks efficiently, enjoying this time with him. Sensing something very special happening. Thrilled to share with him again.

They touched glasses across the desk, and he said, almost jubilantly, "To the Gods, goddam them!"

3

Carole instructed Juanita in the cleaning and preparing of the house. She put old Martin, the head caretaker and yardman, and his two younger sons trimming the garden. This last was unnecessary because old Martin loved the leisure and independence of his job. He kept everything in shape anyway. It did, however, serve its purpose. Carole felt like she was doing *something*. In fact, an excitement she hadn't felt for a long time came upon her. She remembered the first really important entertaining she'd done for Joshua after their marriage. He was on a crucial middle east oil deal.

It was in their New York townhouse in the days they were commuting around the world to various homes and apartments. She had really pulled a coup. Carole had worked closely with the shiek's male secretary and found what to her were some surprising facts. At first she'd intended to have food catered native to the guests' own country and utilize local belly dancers of the same origin. But after much consultation she served hamburgers and had three glowing, local-born blondes as dancing girls. The shieks raved over the Yankee food they'd heard so much about and were obviously taken with the yellow-topped, fair-skinned dancing girls. They were also highly captivated by Carole herself. The whole thing had been a rousing success. Joshua got his oil concessions and she had felt an enormous sense of accomplishment.

Today, as she moved about the vast hacienda she felt some of that old energy returning. There was something different though. Her excitement was mounting, but it was more like one must feel stalking a man-eating tiger and knowing that at the next parting of the bushes they would look into each other's eyes.

Joshua checked out the wine cellar. He loved the silence and the dank smell. He touched some of the ancient casks as he had the history books in the study. He was drawn to old things now, remembering, recalling, conjuring up the history of his land . . . the great southwest. He lingered long after he knew the supply of fine wines was more than sufficient. He moved the lantern back and forth, watching the shadows hide from the moving light. Carole had long wanted him to have electricity installed down here but he'd refused. Some things need to remain as they are, he felt. Many of the old ways were better. Many worse. He'd wondered uncounted times why men who could build computers and fly to distant planets were too blind, or stupid, to select the best of the old and the best of the new and weld them together. He knew that at least the moderate happiness of mankind was that simple. An idiot could see it if he opened up and looked. It would not happen during Joshua's brief encounter with this planet. He knew it and was disgusted by it.

He set the lantern on a shelf and stood gazing at the wall ending the cellar. It was a while before the visions would begin coming to him. He didn't mind. Time was both nothing and everything. Then he heard the hooves of many horses walking methodically forward. It was like the beat of countless drumsticks against the earth. A rhythm, a pattern, a definite purpose in the sound. Closer. Louder. The song came as a sigh at first, then a whisper, finally it was clear and hauntingly lovely. He felt thousands of years old, perhaps millions, perhaps ageless. Colors in circular and elongated patterns danced about in the wall. Slowly they took form as if just being born. Swiftly now they melded into shape and he saw Cortez majestically leading his men and horses in clothing of iron. From the left came Montezuma and his followers in dazzling costumes so wildly colored they appeared to be walking rainbows. They knelt and prostrated themselves to the Gods with four legs. Beauty had bent to force.

Joshua was witnessing the beginning of the Americas. The vision dissolved like a panoramic movie and the song seeped away.

Then Oñate appeared splashing his column across the Rio Grande at the Pueblo of Juarez and headed north up the river. The cellar suddenly reverberated with the swish of a sword into red flesh and there was a huge, moving collage of churning, charging horses, and arrows whistling into the cracks of armor, and many things fell to the earth and became still. Oñate sat astride his horse surveying the compound of a conquered pueblo.

The song came again suddenly, shatteringly, crescendoing as Joshua's Spanish princess stood on a hill looking down. She came towards him, appearing to walk just above the earth. As she neared, smiling, with both arms out, he moved to the wall. As they came closer he reached the wall with his arms outspread trying to physically feel into it, but she was gone. He stayed thusly for a while, his head turned sideways, pushing his whole body against the dirt. For a moment he sagged and took a breath into his body that released him. He turned, picked up the lantern, and zombied his way up to the other world. The one here.

4

All was ready. The tables were filled with every delicacy of the land from which Joshua, his father, and grandfathers twice back had sprouted. The hacienda shined from repeated dusting and polishing. A cantina holding many bottles from many other lands was set up in the main room and an even greater display was waiting for eager hands, dry throats, and tight emotions in the patio.

Carole moved about checking over and over that which was already done. Joshua had one chore left.

"Martin, drain the pool."

CANDLES IN THE BOTTOM OF THE POOL

Martin looked at his master, puzzled. "But sir, the guests will . . ."

"Just drain the pool."

"Well . . . yes sir."

When Carole saw this she hurried to Martin and asked in agitated confusion what in hell madness possessed him to do such a thing.

"It was on orders of Mr. Joshua, madam."

"Then he's mad! We cleaned the pool only yesterday!"

She found Joshua in the study and burst in just as Charlotte finished rechecking her own list and was saying, "Everything has been done, Joshua. The doctors are even releasing Grebbs from the hospital so he can make it."

"Of course, I knew you'd take care of . . ."

"Joshua!"

He turned slowly to her.

"Have you lost all your sanity? Why did you have Martin drain the pool?"

"It's simple, my dear. Pools can become hypnotic and distracting. We have far greater forms of entertainment coming up."

She stood there unable to speak momentarily. She pushed at her hair and rubbed her perspiring palms on her hips, walking in a small circle around the room, finally giving utterance, "*I* know you're crazy, but do you want everyone else to know it?"

"It will give them much pleasure to finally find this flaw in my nature they have so desperately been seeking."

She turned and cascaded from the room, hurling back, "Oh, my God!"

Forty-eight hours later they came from all around the

CANDLES IN THE BOTTOM OF THE POOL

world. They arrived in jets, Rolls Royces, Cadillacs, Mercedes, and pickup trucks. They moved to the hacienda magnetized.

The greetings were both formal and friendly, fearful and cheerful. Carole was at her gracious best, only half drunk, expertly suppressing their initial dread with her trained talk. But there was a difference in the hands and arms and bodies that floated in the air towards Joshua. These appurtenances involved a massive movement of trepidation, hate and fatherhood.

Joshua took Aleta in his grand and strong arms and lifted her from the floor in teasing love and respect. Her husband, Rob, died a little bit right there. His impulse of murder to the being of this man was intensified and verified. Rob wanted *in* desperately. He craved to become part of the Stone domain; craved to be part of the prestige and power. Marrying the favorite niece had seemed the proper first step. It hadn't worked. Joshua had never asked him, and Aleta absolutely forbade Rob to even hint at it. His lean, handsome face had a pinched appearance about it from the hatred. He had dwelled on it so long now that it was an obsession—an obsession to destroy that which he felt had ignored and destroyed him. It was unjustified. Joshua simply didn't want to see Rob subservient to him—not the husband of his artist niece. Aleta had never asked Joshua for anything but his best wishes. He felt that Rob must be as independent as she or else they wouldn't be married. He was wrong. Being a junior partner in a local stock brokerage firm didn't do it for Rob. And their being simply ordered here to Aleta's obvious joy had tilted his rage until he could hardly contain it.

CANDLES IN THE BOTTOM OF THE POOL

Others—who were *in*—felt just as passionately about Joshua, but they all had their separate and different reasons.

Lana and Joseph Helstrom certainly had a different wish for Joshua. Joseph just hadn't moved as high in the organization as swiftly as he felt he should, and Lana had a hidden yen for Joshua. In fact, she often daydreamed of replacing Carole.

And there was the senior vice president, Grebbs, who wanted and believed that Joshua should step up to the position of chairman of the board and allow him his long overdue presidency. He had lately been entering hospitals for check-ups which repeatedly disclosed nothing wrong—but then x-rays do not show hatred or they would have been white with explosions all over his body.

None of these things bothered Joshua now. The gathering grew in momentum of sound, emotion, and color. The drinks consumed along with the food and talk was of many things. People split up into ever-changing groups. Those who had been to the hacienda before remarked about this alteration or that. Those who were new to its centuries made many, many comments about all the priceless objects of art and craft. Whether they hated or loved the master of the house they were somehow awed and honored to be in this museum of the spirit of man and Joshua himself.

Alfredo the guitarist from Juarez played. His dark head bent over his instrument, and the long delicate fingers stroked from the wood and steel the tenderness of love, the savagery of death. It seemed that these songs, too, came from the walls. Maybe somehow they did.

The music surged into the total system of Joshua. He felt stronger, truer than ever before. He was ready now to make his first move—the beginning of his final commitment. He looked about the room, observing with penetration his followers. His eyes settled on Charlotte. And then, as if knowing, unable to resist, she came to him. She handed him a new scotch and water, holding her own drink with practiced care. He turned and she followed at his side. They wandered to the outer confines of the house—to his childhood room. She did not question. He turned on a small lamp that still left many shadows.

"My darling," he said softly, touching the walls with one hand, "this is where it all started."

She looked at him puzzled, but with patience.

"I think I was five when I first heard the walls. It was gunfire and screams and I knew it had once happened here. You see, this, in the days of the vast Spanish land grants, was a roadhouse, a cantina, an oasis where the Dons and their ladies gathered to fight and fornicate. They are in the walls, you know, and I hear them. I even see them. I had just turned thirteen when I first *saw* into the walls."

Joshua's eyes gleamed like a coyote's in lantern light. His breath was growing and there was an electricity charging through all his being. Charlotte was hypnotized at his voice and what was under it. His hand moved down the walls as he told her of some of the things he'd seen and heard. Then he turned to her and raised his glass for a toast.

"To you, dear loyal, wonderful Charlotte, my love and my thanks."

"It has all been a fine trip with you, Joshua. I could not have asked more from life than to have been a part of you and what you've done. Thank you, thank you."

He took the drink from her hand and set it on a dresser.

Taking her gently by the arm he pulled her to the wall. "Now lean against it and listen and you, too, will hear." She did so, straining with all her worth. "Listen! Listen," he whispered, and his powerful hands went around her neck. She struggled very little, and in a few moments she went limp. He held her a brief second longer, bending to kiss her on the back of the neck he'd just broken. Then with much care he picked her up, carried her to the closet, and placed her out of sight behind some luggage. He quietly closed the door, standing there a while looking at it. He moved, picked up his drink, and returned to his people.

5

In the patio, Misha, the Russian dancer from Kavkaz on Sunset Boulevard, was leaping wildly about, crouching, kicking. A circle formed around him and the bulk of Joshua Stone III dominated it all. He was enjoying himself to the fullest, clapping his hands and yelling encouragement. The dance had turned everyone on a few more kilocycles. They started drinking more, talking more and louder, even gaining a little courage.

The grey, fiftyish Grebbs tugged at Joshua, trying to get his true attention. He kept bringing up matters of far flung business interests. He might remind one in attitude of a presidential campaign manager, just after a victory, wondering if he'd be needed now. He rubbed at his crew cut hair nervously, trying to figure an approach to Joshua. His grey eyes darted about slightly. His bone-edged nose presented certain signs of strength and character, but weakness around the mouth gave him away. He was clever and did everything that cleverness could give to keep all underlings out of touch with Joshua. He had hoped for a while that this gathering had been called to announce Joshua's chairmanship, and the fulfillment of his own desperate dream.

Joshua motioned to Lotus Flower, the belly dancer, and she moved gracefully out into the patio ahead of the music. Then the music caught up with her. The Oriental lady undulated and performed the moves that have always pleased men.

As Grebbs tugged at Joshua again, he said, without taking his eyes from the dancer, "Grebbs, go talk business to your dictaphone." Just that. Now Grebbs knew. He moved away, hurting.

Lana stood with Carole. They were both watching Joshua with far different emotions.

Lana spoke first, about their mutual interest. "Has Joshua put on some weight?"

"No, it's the same old stomach."

"He's always amazed everyone with his athletic abilities."

"Really?" This last had a flint edge to it.

"Well, for a man who appears so awkward it is rather surprising to find how swiftly and strongly he can move when he decides to. Carole, you do remember the time he leaped into Spring Lake and swam all the way across it, and then just turned around and swam all the way back. You must remember that, darling. We all had such a good time."

"Oh, I remember many things, *darling.*"

CANDLES IN THE BOTTOM OF THE POOL

Rob was saying to Joseph Helstrom, "There's something wrong here. I feel it. Here it's only September, and he's already drained the pool."

Joseph touched his heavy rimmed glasses and let the hand slowly slide down his round face, "Yeah, he demanded we all come here on instant notice and he's not really with us."

"The selfish bastard." Rob exhaled this like ridding himself of morning spittum.

The dancer swirled ever closer to Joshua, her head back, long black hair swishing across her shoulders. He smiled, absorbed in the movement of flesh as little beams of hatred were cast across the patio from Grebbs, Rob, Joseph—and others. Joshua didn't care—didn't even feel it. As the dance finished, Rob walked out into the garden and removed a small automatic pistol from the back of his belt under his jacket. He checked the breech and replaced the gun.

Joshua worked his way through the crowd, spoken to and speaking back in a distracted manner. His people looked puzzled after his broad back. He made his way slowly down the stairs towards the wine cellar, one hand caressing the wall. He stopped and waited. The song came from eternities away, soft, soothing, amidst the whispers of men planning daring moves.

The whole wall now spun with colors slowly forming into warriors. Then there before Joshua's eyes was Estaban the black man, standing amidst the pueblo Indians. Joshua had always felt that Estaban was one of the most exciting and mysterious—even neglected—figures in the history of America. It has never been settled for sure how or why he arrived in the southwest. However, his influence would always be there. He had started the legend of The Seven

CANDLES IN THE BOTTOM OF THE POOL

Golden Cities of Cibola, which Coronado and many others searched for in vain. He was a major factor in the pueblo rebellion, afterwards becoming the chief of several of these communities. He became a famous medicine man and was looked on as a God. But, like all earthly Gods, he fell. A seven year drought came upon the land of the Tewas, and when he could not dissipate it, he was blamed for it. They killed him and the superstitious Zunis skinned him like a deer to see if he was black all the way through.

Now, at last, Joshua was looking upon this man of dark skin and searing soul as he spoke in the Indian tongue to his worshippers. He talked to them of survival without the rule of iron. They mumbled low in agreement. Maybe Joshua would learn some of the dark secrets before this apparition dissolved back to dried mud.

Joshua watched as up and down the river the Indians threw rock and wood at steel in savage dedication. Men died screaming in agony, sobbing their way painfully to the silence of death. The river flowed peacefully before him now, covering the entire wall and beyond. Then the feet splashed into his view and he saw the remnants of the defeated Spanish straggle across the river back into Mexico.

Joshua's Spanish lady in black lace sat on a smooth, round rock staring across a valley dripping with the gold of autumn. She was in a land he'd never seen. She turned her heel toward him, and gave a smile that said so much he couldn't stand it. He reached towards the wall and she nodded her head up and down and faded away with the music. Silence. More silence. Then,

"Joshua."

He turned. It was Lana. She moved to him, putting her

hands on his chest. "Joshua, what is it? You're acting so strangely."

"Did you see? Did you hear?" he asked, looking out over her head.

"I . . . I . . . don't know what you mean, darling. See what?"

"Nothing. Nothing," he sighed.

"Can I help? Is there *anything* I can do?"

He pulled her against him and kissed her with purpose. She was at first surprised and then gave back to him. He picked her up and shoved her violently against the wooden frame between two wine barrels.

"No, no, not here."

"There is no other time," he said. "No other place." As he reached under her, one elbow struck a spigot on a barrel. He loved her standing there while a thin stream of red wine poured out on the cellar floor forming an immediate pool not unlike blood.

She uttered only one word, "Joshua," and the wine sound continued.

6

Both he and Lana were back among the people now. Carole came to him.

"Where've you been? Where is Charlotte? The phone is ringing constantly. Where is she?"

CANDLES IN THE BOTTOM OF THE POOL

"She's on vacation."

"Today? I can't believe you, Joshua. You always bragged about how she was there when you needed her."

"We don't need her now."

"You really are mad. Mad! Today of all days we need her to answer the phone."

"Take the damned phone off the hook. No one ever calls good news on a phone, anyway. If they have anything good to say, they come and see you personally." He walked away and left her standing there looking after him in much confusion.

All afternoon he had been wanting to visit his old friend, Chalo Gonzales, from the Apache reservation. They met when they were kids. Chalo's father had worked the nearby orchards and alfalfa fields for Joshua's father. He and Chalo hunted, fished, adventured together off and on for years. He'd gone with him to the reservation many times, and learned much of nature and the red man's ways. Chalo had given him as much as anyone—things of real value. He found him dressed in a regular business suit and tie, but he wore a band around his coarse, dark hair.

"Ah, amigo, let's walk in the garden away from this . . ." and he made a gesture with his arm to the scattered crowd. "How does it go with you and your people?"

"Slow, Joshua, but better. As always, there's conflict with the old and the young. The old want to stay with their own ways. The young want to rush into the outside world."

"It's the nature of youth to be impatient. It can't be helped."

"Oh, sure, that is the truth. But our young want to take

the best of the old and good ways with them. They want both sides now. Now."

"That's good, Chalo. They're right."

"But nothing happens that fast. It has been too many centuries one way. You can't change it in a few years."

"It's a big problem I admit, but you will survive and finally win. You always have, you know."

"You've always given me encouragement. I feel better already."

They talked of hunts, and later adventures when they both came home for the summer from school. Chalo had been one of few to make it from his land to Bacone, the Indian college.

Joshua felt Chalo was his equal. He was comfortable with him. They stood together and talked in a far recess of the secluded garden where they could see the mountains they'd so often explored. Joshua felt a surge of love for his old friend. He knew what he must do. He'd spotted the root a few minutes back. He didn't dare risk it with his hands. Chalo was almost as strong as he was in both will and muscle.

He picked up the root and began drawing designs with it in a spot of loose ground, as men will do who are from the earth. Then, as his friend glanced away, Joshua swung it with much force, striking him just back of the ear. He heard the bone crunch and was greatly relieved to know he wouldn't have to do more. Without any wasted time he dragged and pushed him into a thick clump of brush. He checked to see if the body was totally hidden, tossed the root in after it, walked to the wall and looked out across the desert to the mountains again. He was very still; then he turned, smiling ineluctably, and proceeded to the party.

CANDLES IN THE BOTTOM OF THE POOL

7

Dusk came swiftly and hung a while, giving the party a sudden subdued quality. It was the time of day that Joshua liked best. He finally escaped the clutchers and went to his study, locking the door and grinning at the phone Carole had taken off the hook and deliberately dangled across the lamp.

He drew the shades back and sat there absorbed in the hiding sun, and watched the glowing oranges and reds turn to violet and then a soft blue above the desert to the west. He knew that life started stirring there with the death of the sun. The coyotes and bobcats were already moving, sniffing the ground and the air for other living creatures. Many mice, rabbits, and birds would die this night so they could live. The great owl would soon be swooping above them in direct competition. The next day the sun would be reborn and the vultures would dine on any remains, keeping the desert clean and in balance.

Someone knocked on the door. It was Carole.

"Joshua, are you in there?" Then louder, "Joshua, I know you're there because the door is locked from the inside. What are you doing with the door locked anyway?" Silence. "At least you could come and mix with your guests. You did *invite* them, you know." She pounded on the door now. "My God, at least speak to me. I am your wife, you know." Silence. She turned in frustration and stamped off down the hall, mumbling about his madness.

Joshua turned his lounge chair away from the window

CANDLES IN THE BOTTOM OF THE POOL

and stared at the wall across the room. There were things he had to see before he made the final move. Pieces of the past that he must reconstruct properly in his mind before he took the last step.

It did come. As always he heard it first, then saw it form, whirling like pieces of an abstract world—a new world, an old world, being broken and born, falling together again. The Spanish returned. They came now with fresh men, armor, horses, and cannon. They marched and rode up the Rio Grande setting up the artillery, blasting the adobe walls to dust. Then they charged with sabers drawn and whittled the shell-shocked Indians into slavery. They mined the gold from the virgin mountains with the Indians as their tools. And then it all vanished inwardly.

There was quiet and darkness now until he heard his name. "Joshua, Joshua, Joshua." It came floating from afar as if elongated, closer, closer. She was there. He leaned forward in the chair, his body tense, anxious. She stood by a river of emerald green. It was so clear that he could see the separate grains of white sand on its bottom. The trees, trunks thicker than the hacienda, rose into the sky. They went up, up past his ability to see. The leaves were as thick as watermelons and fifty people could stand in the shade of a single leaf. The air danced with the light of four suns shafting great golden beams down through the trees.

She moved towards him through one of the beams and for a moment vanished with its brilliance. Now she was whole again, standing there before him. He ached to touch her. He hurt. An endless string of silver fish swam up the river now. The four suns penetrated the pure water and made them appear to be parts of a metallic lava flow from

CANDLES IN THE BOTTOM OF THE POOL

a far off volcano. But they were fish, moving relentlessly, with no hesitation whatsoever, knowing their destination and fate without doubt.

Again the word came from her as she turned and walked down the river, vanishing behind a tree. "Joshua."

For a fleeting moment he heard the song. He closed his eyes. When he opened them there was just the darkness of the room. He didn't know how long he sat there before returning to the party.

He moved directly to the bar in the patio and ordered a double scotch and water. His people were scattered out now, having dined, and were back into the drinking and talking. The volume was beginning to rise again. It was second wind time. As the bartender served the drink he felt something touch his hand. It was Maria Windsor.

She smiled like champagne pouring, her red lips pulling back over almost startling white teeth. She smiled with her blue eyes, too.

"It has been such a long time," she said.

"Maria, goddamn, it's good to see you." And he hugged her, picking her off the floor without intending to. She was very small and at first appeared to be delicate. But this was a strong little lady. She was a barmaid in his favorite place in El Paso when he first met her. He'd always deeply admired the polite and friendly smoothness with which she did her job. One never had to wait for a drink, the ash tray was emptied at the proper moment, and she knew when to leave or when to stand and chat. Joshua had introduced her to John Windsor, one of his junior vice presidents, and now they were married.

"I love the portrait Aleta did of you."

"Well, I feel embarrassed hanging it there, but what could I do after she worked so hard on it. How are you and John getting along?" he asked.

"How do you mean? Personally or otherwise?"

"Oh, all around I suppose."

"Good," she said. "Like all wives I think he works too hard sometimes, but I suppose that's natural. Here he comes now."

John shook hands and greeted his boss without showing any apparent fear and revealing a genuine liking for him. He once told Maria that he'd love Joshua to his death just for introducing her to him. He was about five eleven, straight and well-muscled, and had thick brown hair which he wore longer than anyone in the whole international organization. He, too, had a nice, white smile.

Joshua ordered a round for the three of them. He raised his glass: "My friends, you'll be receiving a memo in the next few days that I think you will enjoy. Here's to it." Several days before the party Joshua had made out a paper giving John Windsor control of the company. It had not been delivered yet.

He left them glowing in anticipation and went to find his favorite kin, Aleta. As he moved, the eyes of hatred moved with him . . . drunker now, braver. He walked into the garden, bowing, speaking here and there, but not stopping. The moon hung in place by galactic gravity beamed back the sun in a blue softness. The insects and night birds hummed a song in the caressing desert breeze. The leaves on the trees moved just enough to make love. There was a combination of warmth and coolness that only the desert can give.

CANDLES IN THE BOTTOM OF THE POOL

Aleta had seen her uncle and somehow knew he was looking for her. She came to him from where she'd been sitting on a tree that was alive but bent to the ground. She'd been studying the light patterns throughout the garden for a painting she had in mind.

"Uncle Joshua, it's time we had a visit."

He took both her hands and stood back looking at her. "Yes, it's time, my dear. You are even more beautiful than the best of your paintings."

"Well, Uncle, that's not saying much," she said, being pleasingly flattered just the same.

He led her to an archway and opened the iron gate. They walked up a tiny rutted wagon road into the desert. The sounds of the gathering subdued. The yucca bushes and Joshua trees that he'd been named after—speared the sky like frozen battalions of soldiers on guard duty forever.

"Remember when we used to ride up this trail?" she asked.

"Yes, it seems like yesterday."

"It seems like a hundred years ago to me."

He laughed. "Time has a way of telescoping in and out according to your own time. That's the way it should be. You were a tough little shit," he added with fondness. "You were the only one that could ride with me all day."

"That was simple bullheadedness. I knew I was going to be an artist someday and you have to have a skull made of granite to be an artist."

He was amused by her even now. "But you also had a bottom made of rawhide."

They talked of some of her childhood adventures they'd shared. Then the coyotes howled off in a little draw. The strollers stood like the cacti, listening, absorbing the oldest cry left.

When the howls stopped, he spoke: "I love to hear them. I always have. I even get lonely to hear them. They're the only true survivors."

"That somehow frightens me," she said with a little shudder.

"It shouldn't. You should be encouraged. As long as they howl, people have a chance here on earth. No longer, no less. It is the final cry for freedom. It's hope."

They walked on silently for a spell. "You really are a romantic, Uncle. When I hear people say how cold you are I laugh to myself."

"You know, Aleta darling, you're the only person that never asked me for anything?"

"I didn't have to. You've always given me love and confidence. What more could you give?"

"I don't know. I wish I did."

"No, Uncle, there's no greater gift than that."

"Aleta, the world is strange. Mankind has forgotten what was always true—that a clean breath is worth more than the most elegant bank building. A new flower opening is more beautiful than a marble palace. All things rot. Michelangelo's sculpture is even now slowly breaking apart. All empires vanish. The largest buildings in the world will turn back to sand. The great paintings are cracking, the negatives of the best films ever made are right now losing their color and becoming brittle. The tallest mountains are coming down a rock at a time. Only thoughts live. You are only what you think."

CANDLES IN THE BOTTOM OF THE POOL

"That's good," she said; "then I'm a painting, even if I am already beginning to crack."

He liked her words and added some of his own: "You know, honey, the worms favor the rich."

"Why?"

He rubbed his great belly. "Because they're usually fatter and more easily digestible."

"Do you speak of yourself?"

"Of course," he smiled. The coyotes howled again, and he said, "I love you, my dear Aleta."

"And I love you."

He stroked her hair and moved his hand downward. It had to be swift, clean. With all his strength, even more than he'd ever had before. He grabbed her long, graceful neck and twisted her head. He heard the bones rip apart. She gasped only once and then a long sigh of her last breath exuded from her. He gathered her carefully in his arms and walked out through the brush to the little draw where the coyotes had so recently hunted. Then he stretched her out on the ground with her hands at her side and gently brushed her hair back. She slept in the moonlight.

He walked swiftly back to the hacienda. As he left the garden for the patio, Rob stepped in front of him.

"Joshua, have you seen Aleta?"

"Of course, my boy, of course."

"Well, where is she?"

"Look, I don't follow your wife around. She's certainly more capable than most of taking care of herself." Joshua moved on. Rob followed him a few steps, looking at his back with glazed eyes.

Grebbs grabbed at him in one last desperate hope that Joshua was saving the announcement to the last.

"Joshua, I have to talk with you. Please."

Joshua stopped and looked at the man. He was drunk, and that was something Grebbs rarely allowed himself to be in public. He looked as if pieces of flesh were about to start dropping down into his clothing. His mouth was open, slack and watery.

Joshua said, with a certainty in his voice that settled Grebbs' question, "Grebbs, you're a bad drinker. I have no respect for bad drinkers." And he moved on.

Grebbs stared at the same back the same way Rob had. He muttered, actually having trouble keeping from openly crying, "The bastard. The dirty bastard. I'll kill you! You son of a bitch!"

The thing some of these people had been uttering about Joshua now possessed them. A madness hovered about, waiting for the right moment, and then swiftly moved into them. Now all the people of music started playing at once. The Russian was dancing even more wildly, if not so expertly. The belly dancer swished about from man to man, teasing. The Mariachis walked about in dominance for a while, then the brass group would break through. It was a cacophony of sound that entered the heads of all there . . . throbbing like blood poison.

Carole started sobbing uncontrollably. Lana began cursing her husband Joseph in vile terms—bitterly, with total malice. Joseph just reached out and slapped her down across the chaise lounge, and a little blood oozed from the corner of her mouth. He could only think of a weapon, any weapon to use on the man who he felt was totally responsible for the matrix of doom echoing all around. We always must have something to hate for our own failures and smallness. But this did not occur to Joseph, or Lana, or Carole, or the others. Only Alfredo the guitarist sat alone on the same old bent tree that Aleta had cherished, touching his guitar with love.

Maria took John aside and told him they were leaving, that something terrible was happening. She was not—and could not be—a part of it. He hesitated but listened. They did finally drive away, confused, but feeling they were right.

Grebbs dazedly shuffled to the kitchen looking for a knife, but old Juanita and her two sisters were there. He then remembered an East Indian dagger that lay on the mantle in the library as a paperweight. In his few trips to the hacienda he'd often studied it, thinking what a pleasure it would be to drive it into the jerking heart of Joshua Stone III.

He picked it up and pulled the arched blade from the jeweled sheath. He touched the sharp unused point with shaking fingers. At that precise instant Rob felt in the back of his belt and touched the automatic. He removed it and put it in his jacket pocket. Joseph Helstrom looked about the patio for an instrument to satisfy his own destructive instincts.

Joshua entered the door to the cellar, shut it, and shoved the heavy iron bolt into place. He called on all his resources now in another direction. An impolsion to the very core of time struck Joshua. Now, right now, he must visualize all the rest of the history of his land that occurred before his first childish awareness. Then, and only then, could he make his last destined move. It began to form. The long lines of

CANDLES IN THE BOTTOM OF THE POOL

Conestoga wagons tape-wormed across the prairies and struggled through the mountain passes bringing goods and people from all over the world to settle this awesome land. They came in spite of flood, droughts, blizzards, Indian attacks and disease. They were drawn here by the golden talk of dreamers, and promising facts.

The ruts of the Santa Fe Trail were cut so deep they would last a century. The mountain men took the last of the beaver from the sweet, churning waters of the mountains above Taos and came down to trade, to dance the wild fandangos, to drink and pursue the dark-eyed lovelies of that village of many flags.

A troop of cavalry charged over the horizon into a camp of Indians and the battle splashed across the adobe valleys in crimson. Thousands of cattle and sheep were driven there and finally settled into their own territories. Cowboys strained to stay aboard bucking horses, and these same men roped and jerked steers, thumping them hard against the earth. They gambled and fought and raised hell in the villages of deserts and mountains, creating written and filmed legends that covered the world more thoroughly than Shakespeare.

The prospectors walked over the mountains searching for—and some finding—large deposits of gold, silver and copper. And, as always, men of money took away the rewards of their labors and built themselves great palaces.

And Joshua saw the Italians, Chinese, and many other nationalities driving the spikes into the rail ties. The trains came like the covered wagons before them—faster, more powerful—hauling more people and goods than ever before. The double-bitted axes and two-man saws cut the majestic

CANDLES IN THE BOTTOM OF THE POOL

pines of the high places, taking away the shelter of the deer, lion and bear.

Now Joshua closed his eyes, for he knew all the rest. When he opened them he heard the song begin again. It was both older and newer each time he heard it. There was a massive adobe church and his lady walked right through the walls and into the one he sat staring at. Now as she spoke his name, he knew his final move was near. For the first time he turned away from her and headed for the door. She smiled, somehow exactly like the song.

As he opened the door and pulled it shut, he felt a presence come at him. He was so keyed up, so full of his feelings, that he just stepped aside and let it hurtle past. It was Grebbs. He'd driven the dagger so deep into the door that he couldn't pull it out to strike again. Grebbs had missed all the way. Joshua gathered him up around the neck with one hand, jerked the dagger from the door with the other, and smashed him against the wall. He shoved the point of the dagger just barely under the skin of Grebbs' guts. Grebbs' eyes bulged and he almost died of fright right there, but the hand of his master cut any words off. It was quite a long moment for the corporate vice president.

"What I should do, Grebbs, is cut your filthy entrails out and shove them down your dead throat. But that's far too easy for you."

Joshua dropped him to the floor and drove the knife to the hilt in the door. He then strode up the stairs three at a time, hearing only a low broken sob below him.

As he entered the world of people again, Carole grabbed at him, visibly drunk and more. She said, "God! God! What are you doing?" He moved on from her as she shrieked,

"You don't love me!" He ignored this too, and when she raked her painted claws into the back of his neck he ignored that as well. She stood looking at her fingers and the bits of bloody flesh clinging to her nails.

Rob blocked his way, again demanding attention. "I'm asking you for the last time! Do you hear me? Where is Aleta?"

He pushed the young man aside, saying as he went, "I'll tell you in a few minutes." This surprised and stopped Rob right where he stood.

Then Joshua raised his arms and shouted, "Music, you fools! Play and dance!" The drunken musicians all started up again, jerky, horrendously out of synchronization.

Joshua went to the kitchen and very tenderly lifted an exhausted and sleeping Juanita from her chair. He explained to her two sisters that he would take Juanita to her room on the other side of the hacienda. They were glad and went on cleaning up. He led her slowly out a side door. On the other side of many walls could be heard the so-called music sailing up, dissipating itself in the peaceful desert air.

As he walked the bent old woman along he spoke to her softly, "It's time for you to rest, Juanita. You've been faithful all these decades. Your sisters can do the labors. You will have time of your own now. A long, long time that will belong just to you. You've served many people who did not even deserve your presence."

There was an old well near the working shed where her little house stood. They stopped here.

"Juanita, you are like this—this dried-up well. It gave so much for so long it now has no water left."

He pulled the plank top off. Juanita was weary and still

CANDLES IN THE BOTTOM OF THE POOL

partially in the world of sleep. Joshua steadied the bony old shoulders with both his hands. He looked at her in the moonlight and said, "Juanita, you are a beautiful woman."

She twitched the tiniest of smiles across her worn face and tiled her head just a little in an almost girlish move.

Then he said, "Juanita, I love you." He slipped a handkerchief from his pocket, crammed it into her mouth, jerked her upside down and hurled her head first into the well. There was just a crumpled thud. No more.

In the patio the music was beginning to die. A dullness had come over the area. A deadly dullness. But heads started turning, one, two, three at a time towards the hacienda door. Their center of attention, Joshua, stode amongst them. There were only whispers now. Joshua saw a movement and stopped. The heavy earthen vase smashed to bits in front of him. He looked up and there on a low wall stood Helstrom like a clown without makeup. He, too, had missed.

Joshua grabbed him by both legs and jerked him down against the bricks of the patio floor. He hit and his head bounced. Joshua gripped him by the neck and the side of one leg and tossed him over and beyond the wall.

He turned slowly around, his eyes covering all the crowd. No one moved. Not at all. He walked back through them to the house and in a few moments returned. He carried a huge silver candelabra, from the first Spanish days, with twenty lighted candles. He walked with it held high. None moved except to get out of his way. Alfredo sat on the edge of the empty pool. His feet dangled down into its empty space. He tilted his head the way only he could do and softly, so very softly, strummed an old Spanish love song—a song older than the hacienda. Joshua walked to the steps of the pool and with absolute certainty of purpose stepped carefully down into it. It seemed a long time, but it was not. He placed the candelabra in the deepest part of the pool, stepped back, and looked into the flames. Then he raised his head and stared upwards at all the faces that now circled the pool to stare down at him. He turned in a complete circle so that he looked into the soft reflections in each of their eyes. He saw all things in that small turn. None of them knew what *they* were seeing. He walked back up the steps and there stood Rob.

Joshua said, "Come now, Rob, and I'll tell you what you really want to know."

Alfredo went on singing in Spanish as if he was making quiet love. The circle still looked downwards at the glowing candles.

Near the largest expanse of wall on the whole of the hacienda, Joshua said quietly to Rob, "I killed her. I took her into the desert and killed sweet Aleta."

Rob was momentarily paralyzed. Then a terrible cry and sound of murder burst from him as he ripped the edge of his pocket pulling out the gun. He fired right into the chest of Joshua, knocking him against the wall. He pulled at the trigger until there was nothing left. Joshua stayed upright for a moment, full of holes, and then fell forward, rolling over face up. The crowd from the pool moved towards Rob, hesitantly, fearfully. They made a half circle around the body.

Rob spoke, not looking away from Joshua's dead, smiling face as if afraid he'd rise up again, "He killed Aleta."

Grebbs, saying things unintelligible like a slavering idiot, pushed his way through the mass, stopping with his face above Joshua's. Then he vented a little stuttering laugh.

CANDLES IN THE BOTTOM OF THE POOL

It broke forth louder and louder, and haltingly the others were caught up with him. They laughed and cried at the same time, not knowing really which they were doing. None thought to look at the wall above the body. It didn't matter, though, for all those who might have seen were already there. On a thin-edged hill stood Charlotte the dedicated, Aleta the beloved, Chalo the companion, and old Juanita the faithful. They were in a row, smiling with contentment. Just below them the lady in black lace walked forward to meet Joshua.

As he moved into the wall there came from his throat another form of laughter that far, far transcended the hysterical cackling in the patio. He glanced back just once and the song overcame his mirth. He took her into his arms and held her. They had waited so very long. It was over. They walked, holding hands, up the hill to join those he loved, and they all disappeared into a new world.

The wall turned back to dirt.

None could stay at the hacienda that night. Just before the sun announced the dawn, the last candle in the bottom of the pool flickered out. The light was gone.